S0-DQV-803

THE LOST SKIFF

DONALD WETZEL

SECOND CHANCE PRESS
SAG HARBOR, NEW YORK

To

our friends

Marvin and Martha Nichols

and family

David and Jane Abts

Copyright © 1969 by Donald Wetzel, © 1985 by Second Chance Press
All rights reserved. No part of this publication may be reproduced or
transmitted in any form or by any means, electronic or mechanical, in-
cluding photocopy, recording, or any information storage and retrieval
system, without permission in writing from the publisher.
First edition
Library of Congress Catalog Card Number: 85-061541
ISBN: 0-933256-60-4 (cloth)
      0-933256-61-2 (paper)
Printed in the United States of America

Other books by Donald Wetzel

A Wreath and a Curse

The Age of Light

The Rain and the Fire and the Will of God

The Obscenity

Forward

by Mark Harris

Donald Wetzel is our prophet. He has always, at any rate, been mine these forty years, since first I set eyes upon him on the street in Albuquerque where we then lived. He was in the company of his tall, blond, handsome, achieving cousin who was carrying a little dog in the pocket of his great jacket.

Wetzel was starting out as a writer, though he couldn't spell, so that he came to be not only a prophet but living proof that you needn't know how to spell to write. (We had a dear friend in Denver named Gladys, whose possessive form Wetzel spelled "Glady's".) Writing is not spelling but feeling.

Wetzel was well-acquainted with the work of William Faulkner at a time when I had scarcely heard the name. Faulkner was then *avant garde* and almost unknown. Wetzel also loved classical music, for which I had no ear; and his eyes saw natural things where I saw only cities. In those ways, and in others, he was in advance of me, and he existed as well as teacher and model for me, walking about with an advanced case of moral sensibility which is still in advance of the moral sense which governs us from the capitals.

Our lives crossed and re-crossed in many places beyond Albuquerque. We went off in all directions, though not at once. In Denver, with wives and others, we shared a house dear to my memory. I wrote something of that period in a book: "Once I heard a child say to him, 'You're rather bald,' and him reply, 'Honey, I'm *damn* bald.' In a house we shared in Denver his room adjoined my wife's and mine, and when we heard his alarm clock ring we waited with amusement for the two sounds to follow: first, Wetzel's striking a match, and then, after his first puff of

I

cigarette, the utterance, 'Shit!' For Wetzel the day had begun, overhung always with a tragic sense of life I did not then understand or share. He was a white Protestant Southerner with every advantage but the capacity to make deals with society. He knew, above all, in war or civil life, that one became what one did, that process was all, method was all, men reaped what they sowed."

He lives now in Bisbee, Arizona, one of those towns attractive to younger artists in preference to the hustling life of the cities. It is the kind of town Wetzel has usually chosen. The artists who live there are never our conventionally achieving cousins. His living-room matters to him. Early in our acquaintance Wetzel wrote a story whose truth of prophesy is clear enough now. It was a tale, as I recall, of someone making a weapon too big for safe-keeping; so he roped off an area somehow; but that wasn't enough, either — he needed more space; he roped off the whole town, the county, the state, and ended by roping or fencing or walling the whole State of Texas. Now there was room safely to house the weapon.

Off the road near Albuquerque and Santa Fe things were going on at Los Alamos. This was 1947. We saw the distant lights at night, but we weren't supposed to know what was going on. We hadn't been cleared for loyalty by the people who did, or thought they did. But Wetzel the prophet knew what was going on and knew it was bad and knew the time would come when we'd run out of the space to contain it.

A second story of Wetzel's comes to mind. He has recently written it. I heard it forty years ago. It was based on this: Wetzel, some time in the early 1940's, was held in jail pending his transfer to a Federal prison housing conscientious objectors to World War Two. In jail he shared space with one of the leading criminals of the era, who was later executed at Sing Sing, New York. The criminal, as it happens, was a Jew, and in the confidence of his scholarship he perceived Wetzel as a Jew. He undertook to scold Wetzel for having resisted military service. Every good Jew should be out fighting the Nazis. The famous criminal deplored pacifists.

Well, don't worry, the State punished Wetzel even if the righteous criminal could not. Because of his pacifism Wetzel was deprived of many rights and privileges accorded those of us who

II

had entered military service and more or less served. I was one who entered, served glumly for awhile, and at some point during the experience began to apprehend the danger of it all both to my body and to my moral sense or reason. Soon after leaving military service, meeting Wetzel, I was able to begin to form arguments against the idea of military power. I had had no language, philosophy, or model to support my instincts. It was Wetzel who drew from me the English to describe those emotions I had so privately sheltered during that period of solitude when I was surrounded by millions of men making great noise. I had known no cultural or intellectual setting for my fantasy.

Wetzel's was a service to me for which I soon expressed my gratitude. In a novel of my own I created a character, a young baseball player, who preferred his own Coward Crouch to the idea of fighting. I dedicated my novel to Wetzel who, on the other hand, odd as it now seems to me, must have felt some sort of gratitude to me as well, for he soon dedicated *his* first novel to *me*. It was more than merely *quid pro quo*. It was a thing we felt. We were important to each other. I mention this to clear the air of accusations of conflict of interest. We have long been friends and cannot deny it.

The world is catching up with Wetzel. *Stop*, it now begins to say, *you are fencing the weapon in and the human being out, outer space is a military base*. Of *The Lost Skiff* Wetzel has written, "I feel that the little book might speak now to a mood in the country favorable to a reawakening sense of where we, humankind, fit in the planet earth's scheme of things. . ." This is not to say that the book is simply programmatic. In any simple sense Wetzel never has had a program, although no careful reader will find difficulty in discerning general directions in his work. He has expressed ideas of healing and preserving as opposed to wantonness and destruction, ideas of loyalty and fidelity as opposed to savagery and opportunism, ideas respectful of Nature in a world where human beings are Nature's allies, not Nature's conqueror in the ancient *macho* tradition. It is "my personal feeling," he has written, "that our awareness of our reliance upon and ties with all else that lives on this earth is essential to our sanity and survival as a species...that's what I think, and so there!"

It has been Wetzel's achievement that he has never relinquished the clarity of the boy he was in the moment of our meeting so long ago on the street in Albuquerque. From that moment forward he preserved not only himself but certainly me from the suicidal sophistication of the consenting patriot. My wife and I and others of our young circle lived with Wetzel through the struggles of composition of his first novel, *A Wreath and a Curse,* which he wrote in Albuquerque and continued in Denver. During part of the Denver period he supported himself as a hotel clerk. He is still sometimes a hotel clerk. The job is congenial to him, affording him opportunity for conversation and observation, human beings arriving and departing. Once he worked in Denver for a real-estate lady. Wetzel was her telephone-answering machine. The lady otherwise employed women only and had placed an unfortunate advertisement in the Denver directory — LET OUR GIRLS SERVICE YOU. Word soon got around town that the lady's business was prostitution, and it destroyed her. When her business failed as a victim of rumor Wetzel had no choice but to find another job, carrying the truth away with him.

Because I lived so intimately with its makings I seem to remember *A Wreath and a Curse* better than any of Wetzel's other books. He has not necessarily been wiser than he was at the beginning, but in *The Lost Skiff* he has told the story more richly, more subtly, and no doubt more indirectly. Here at the center of his story, as in *A Wreath and a Curse,* is a boy who is as innocent as a boy is bound to be in spite of everything: even in spite of his Star Roamer short-wave radio on which he listens to the world.

Willie, in *A Wreath and a Curse,* attempts to fortify his home against a flooding river. The boy, free of adult preoccupations, was first and quickest among his family to admit the danger of their destruction. We cannot say simply of *The Lost Skiff* that it, too, is a story of a boy, a family, a river. It is exactly "about" those things except that no immediate, apparent danger confronts anyone. Nobody will really be hurt here (one broken wrist), no house will be swept away, nor is the owner of the skiff absolutely desperate for its return. The very tone is of attention not to

IV

calamity but to that action of the boy which might seem to anyone else to be pointless: why seek the lost skiff?

The boy seeks the skiff, I suppose, because he cannot do otherwise than seek it. He remains faithful to some vision of his own. He knows best. Frost has said we know best at nineteen, but Rodney is only fourteen in an age of precocity, an uncorrupted boy whose instinct is to keep the faith, to preserve his own honor, to obey the command nobody has issued except him to himself.

I mean to say that this is not a pious book but a true book, or so it seems to me. Its action is supported by detail, for the boy knows, as his creator knows, how to live with the landscape, travel in terms of approaching storms, permit himself to abandon himself to tides and wind as they assist him. The enemy is not Nature but our arrogance when we defy it. The boy savors nature as at one point he savors the odor of breakfast cooking. He is moving to me. I row with him up or down the river in search of the object he may never find, and I may understand — as he may not yet — how the experience of quest transcends forever the merely missing hard object.

THE LOST SKIFF

1

It was the lousy blue jays that woke me up. Sleeping on an open back porch the way I do, it was like they were screaming right in my ear, although I looked and they were all screaming and hopping around way over in the sand pear trees on the other side of the yard. There must have been a dozen of them, all yelling *Kat, Kat Kat,* in that loud raspy way they have, and kind of jumping up and down on the branches like something had got all of them mad as hell and they were having temper tantrums. If it hadn't been so early it might have seemed funny, even. But it was hardly light, and by habit I am no early bird, and I did not appreciate being waked up from a sound sleep by such crazy loud early birds as these. But they kept it up and even got louder it seemed; *Kat, Kat Kat,* like it was a kind of swear word and the only one they knew. Then I looked, and sure enough, there was one of my uncle's pitiful, half-starved little orange-colored cats—only he says they are not his, but strays—trying to slink up along the path from the barnyard to the house. I doubt if that poor cat could have hurt a one of these jays if he wanted to, but that was what all that ridiculous *Kat* screaming was about. Then the noise was too much, I guess, and the cat turned off the path and slunk in under the grape arbor and then into a bunch of weeds and brambles, and the jays all shut up at once, like someone had thrown a switch.

Seemed like an awful big fuss about nothing, but who knows, maybe to a blue jay cats, any cats, are the world's number one finks. Or maybe there were some baby jays in the bunch, just getting a lesson in how to cuss out a cat. The ways of nature are not my specialty. In fact nothing in Alabama is. I'm a stranger here, more or less. The longer I stay doesn't

3

seem to help much, either. Well, I had learned, anyhow, that Alabama blue jays are probably cat protestors second to none, which is a piece of information hardly worth getting up at daybreak to acquire.

Especially since I had stayed awake late the night before plugged in to Radio Free Cuba—do they ever hate our guts— on my short wave set, listening to this fellow trying to sound as mad talking English with a Spanish accent—which has a nice sound to it, I think, no matter what the words—as he would sound if he were shouting away in straight Spanish. I get some of this, too, sometimes, when I can find Cuba—close as it is, it strays a lot, on my set anyhow—and while I don't understand a word of it, it generally sounds like someone is catching hell. Probably the U. S. of A. My set is a five-band Star Roamer which I paid forty dollars for and then assembled myself. It came to me as nineteen pounds of electronic junk. That it works at all amazes me. The first time I plugged it in and turned it on, I went clean across the room from it and waited for it to either burst into flame or detonate. By some crazy luck, not only did it not go up in smoke or little pieces, but it was right on the right frequency on band three to pick up a ham, loud and clear, that lived about six blocks down the street from me. I'd flipped the volume on full, and this idiot down the street nearly blasted me out of the room bragging to some fellow up in Canada about his African violets, of all things. That was back in White Plains, New York, where I live most of the time.

Here on The Hill, in Alabama, where I am now, my Aunt Vera can't stand the squeaks and squawks the set now and then just naturally makes, so I always use the phone, the earphones, when I listen, and this way I can lie in bed and listen as late at night as I please. Anyhow, because of the jays waking me, I turned the set on and went to band two, which is regular radio, and listened to some music for a while to get the sound of the jays out of my mind. That's how I happened to be awake when Jack Haywood came over from his house across the road and came pounding up the steps and slammed open the screen door and came on in on the porch without knock-

4

ing, the way he always does. Some people have a habit of slamming doors wherever they go, but Jack is the only one I have run across yet who slams them open as well as shut. Well, you know when he's coming or going anyhow.

The bed where I sleep is all the way across the porch from the door, and after Jack had let the door slam shut behind him, he stood there a minute without moving—I could tell he wasn't moving, because if he had of been I would have heard him, even with my earphones on and some outfit worse than the Monkees singing in my ears. Just for the hell of it I kept my eyes closed. Then I heard him say, "You still asleep?" I didn't answer, and then I heard him walking toward me and felt the porch shaking a little. It's a porch my uncle added onto the house, and it shakes easy, although Jack Haywood is big and a heavy walker, even for a country boy, and can make about any floor except a cement one shake a little if he wants to. I lay there looking up at the ceiling with my eyes shut, breathing as shallow as I could, trying to look dead. For a while Jack must have just stood there staring down at me, and then, like he was talking to himself, except loud, he said, "Holy cow!"

Ever since the first time Jack tried my earphones on right after I came down from White Plains he's been scared of my Star Roamer set. I hadn't checked it out good from the trip and he claimed it had shocked his ears, an electric shock. I doubt it, but I hadn't had it grounded right at the time, so maybe it did. So I waited, and Jack finally said "Holy cow" again, and then he said, "I can hear the music. Can you hear me?" Then I laughed and opened my eyes, and Jack laughed, too. "I didn't think you was asleep," Jack said, "and if you had finally electrocuted yourself it seems to me that would have at least shut the music off, too. You give me a scare for a minute though, lying there like a corpse. Hey, you don't sleep with electricity going through your ears all night, do you?" Jack talks like that. I mean his grammar is rotten. It's so bad sometimes I suspect that he talks that way on purpose, like if you woke him up in the middle of the night he would forget and talk pretty much like anyone else. But I'm probably wrong about that. It's just habit, I guess. "Is it true you still sleep with a teddy bear?" I said.

Jack laughed again. He laughs easy, I'll say that for him. "Is it true you haven't stopped wetting the bed yet?" he said, and then he laughed like that was the funniest thing he had ever thought of, and it probably was.

I took off the earphones and shut off the set and sat up in bed and stretched, and then I told Jack about the jays waking me, and that if it hadn't have been them I could see it would have soon been him, and what did he want? He had pulled up a chair by the bed and was studying my radio, the way he often does, as though if he just sits there and looks at it long enough he will understand how I could put a thing like that together when he cannot even figure out how to make it work. The only times he has tried, all he has come up with is squeals and squawks. That set really bugs him, but he won't admit it. "Jays can be a nuisance," he said, still looking at the set. "They're noisy almost any time of the year, but especially now, when they have the new young birds out with them. Then they get fierce, especially if they see an owl or a snake. They can get so excited that I have seen them call up all kinds of other birds, too, mockers, redbirds, thrashers, even little old titmouses and Carolina wrens. I heard them once last year, about this time, right down in your uncle's lot, and I thought sure it must be an owl or a snake, and I took my rifle and ran down there, and I never saw so many different kinds of birds making a fuss at one time in my life."

"No kidding," I said. Jack will always top me if he can.

"What it was was a sparrow hawk," Jack said, "and all he was doing was sitting in a pine tree trying to pick some number-six shot out of his self where someone had shot him from too far off. You could see him sitting up there just pecking away at himself. So I shot him, and took him up to the house and got a knife and pried around enough to satisfy my curiosity. It was number-six shot and he was full of it. But naturally the jays could not have knowed such a thing. And not everybody else would have knowed it, either. The only time jays get quiet is in the spring, when they get ready to

6

raise some more jays. Then they slip off in pairs and that's the last you hear of them until about now. They don't really slip off, but they don't only get quiet, they get hard to see. It's the kind of thing you can't help but notice, like they have all flew off or dropped dead."

"What they saw this morning was one of my uncle's cats," I said.

"Then they had nothing to fear if they only knowed it," Jack said. "Not from one of those poor creatures." Sometimes the words Jack uses wrong can make me wince, but still, what he had told me about jays was news to me all right and probably the truth. Jack wouldn't go to the trouble to lie. It looked like Jack had forgotten about me, and then he shook his head at the radio like he was giving up on it for the time being and got up from the chair. "Well," he said, "I reckon you had planned to lie in bed until noon listening in on China, but in about a half an hour we're going up to The Landing and fix up the boats like we should have done last fall, if you want to come."

"Way up there?" I said.

"What's distance to you?" Jack said. He looked at the radio and shook his head. "Anyhow, we ain't planning to walk."

Last summer, when I came to The Hill for the first time, we had gone up to The Landing once, and about all I could remember about it was a long, hot dusty trip over dirt roads in the back of their pickup, being bounced around on that hot steel truck bottom until I felt like some kid caught in a clothes dryer, and then getting to this little river, which was deeper than it was wide, it seemed to me, and black, where I couldn't see the bottom and sure as hell didn't want to jump in and see if I could find it with my feet, the way Jack kept trying to do. What I remembered most about it, if I am going to be honest, was the mosquitoes, which Jack said were bad that year, and Jack's sister, Ellen, who was seventeen, first scaring me half to death by threatening to push me off The Landing pier, and then wrestling with me about it much more than I was used to wrestling with older girls in bathing suits, and scaring me more this way than the river scared me, so that I jumped in. I

7

came up, still plenty worried about the kind of crazy river I was swimming in, and then Ellen dove in, neat and white and hardly making a splash and came up right in front of me and blew some bubbles at me and then said, "Don't be scared," and after that I wasn't. I remembered that most of all.

"Is Ellen going?" I said. I was still not too wide awake or I wouldn't have said that.

Jack grinned a little, but that was all. "I believe she has some such plans," he said. "Anyhow, she sent me to ask you. Otherwise I might have let you sleep. Growing boys need sleep, Ma says, especially skinny ones. But I forgot, we will be staying overnight, and maybe China cannot be spared having you mind its business for so long a time."

I have never yet been able to raise China on my set, and Jack knows it. I got out of bed and switched on the set and handed Jack the phones. "Why don't you fool around while I get dressed," I said, "and see if you can't electrocute yourself." I got dressed and went into the kitchen, where Aunt Vera was fixing breakfast, and told her I was going up to The Landing with the Haywoods. Then I ate and came back out on the porch, and Jack was sitting there, sweating, with the earphones all the way on, for a change, and a big stupid smile on his face. "Hey," he said, "I reckon I got Russia this time for sure." I took the phones and held them to my ear. Jack had a fine bunch of squeaks and squawks, faint, but clear. I listened a minute and then shut off the set. "That was Russia, all right," I said. "Only it was Siberia. What you heard was the wolves howling in the snow."

"No wonder I couldn't understand it," Jack said, and then he watched me putting a bunch of clean underwear and clothes and my swimming trunks in my United Air Lines bag and he said, "Holy cow"—his mother has really got him trained not to swear—"holy cow, we are not leaving the country, you know, just camping out for the night."

And then I said a dumb thing, which shows how my mind works sometimes, too slow for my big mouth, I mean, as I had already asked Jack once if Ellen was going, but that was before I had known we would be camping out together, and

8

somehow this made it another matter, so to speak, so I said, "Ellen, too?" Camping out, I meant.

Jack looked at me and shook his head like I was a sad case. "Well," he said, speaking slow and phony the way he will do when he thinks he has got something clever to say, "I haven't said nothing to Ellen about it, but I more or less figured you and me would be camping off by ourselves somewhere." Then he just stood there grinning at me like he knew he had just read something dirty in my mind. And what bothered me about that was that if he had been right—and he wasn't, not really—then he shouldn't have been grinning like that because after all it was his own grown sister I had been thinking about. There are some things I don't understand about Jack Haywood. Maybe even most things.

But all I said was, "Ha, ha, you are a real comic, you are," and then I took some of my clothes back out of the bag and said, "Well, I guess there will not be much of a place to change clothes there at that." I have noticed that I never say just one stupid thing at a time.

"Only the whole woods," Jack said, "although if you are worried I can ask Ma and Ellen to hide their eyes." Then I guess Jack saw that I was starting to get mad, although the truth was I was getting mad at myself, not Jack. While Jack is big and can be rough and in most cases is about as subtle as a train wreck, there is nothing mean about him. Anyhow, I guess he saw me going white a little, which I am told is what I do when I get angry, so he laughed and gave me a shot which was meant to be friendly but which felt like it broke my arm, and I gave him a good sharp elbow in the gut, which he pretended for a while was surely a fatal blow—he can be a clown, when he wants to, but I happen to know that about the only thing that could knock the wind out of him would be a fall from a two-story roof—and then we heard his father honking the horn of the pickup across the road and we ran over and jumped in the back.

Ellen was already there, I noticed. She could have ridden up front with her father and mother. But she was sitting in back on a big piece of folded canvas and she smiled and said there

9

was room on it for me, too, so I sat down next to her. "Well,"
I said, "I see you are going to be riding back here with us
delinquents."

"I guess I'm still a kid myself," Ellen said.

Truth is, much as I like her, Ellen is not always too subtle
either. That was kind of like the shot to the arm Jack had
given me. It was meant friendly, but I happen to be two years
younger than she is; still a kid. But then she said, "I like
riding in back, rough and windy as it is. Seems like you see the
country better. Like it just goes sailing by. And anyhow, I
haven't seen you to talk to any length of time for a week now,
at least." I thought that was a nice thing to say, and I believed
that she meant what she said about liking to ride in back. I
remembered from last summer, and if you don't mind the
dust, the country does seem to go sailing by in a nice way at
that. Then Ellen noticed my United Air Lines bag and she
said, "But I suppose the country is most beautiful of all when
you see it floating down there under you from an airplane, like
a bird. Do you have to buy the bag, too, or does that come with
the ticket?"

I had flown down this time, from New York to Mobile, on
United. My opinion of flying was not quite like Ellen's. I
hadn't thought I would be scared, but when I got up there
and looked down and *realized* it, there was something in my
bones, it seemed, telling me that I wasn't brother to any birds
or any kind of angel, but just a boy in one hell of an unnatural place for a boy or any sort of man to be. "I'd sooner see
the country from the back of your pickup," I said. "Any time.
They only give you the bag when you're flying out of the
country, I think. Anyhow, this is one they gave my father once.
All they gave me was some propaganda about how safe it was
to fly and how I'd love it."

"You didn't really like it?" Ellen said.

I guess it wouldn't have hurt anything if I'd said I liked it,
but then later I probably would have forgotten and told them
the truth anyhow, so all I said was, "What I liked most of all
was getting here."

Ellen looked at me a minute and then she smiled and said,

10

"You are a funny one, honest. Any other kid would have naturally said he loved it. Whether he did or not."

Well, I thought, if I am going to be a funny kid I might as well be a good and funny kid. "I was scared stiff the whole damn time," I said.

"Ha," Jack said. "I bet you was." I didn't answer, and then Jack's mother came down finally and got in front with Mr. Haywood and Jack yelled for us to fasten our seat belts, and then Mr. Haywood backed over the cattle guard and Jack hollered, "Blast off," and Ellen shook her head at him like she pitied him. Then we went bouncing up the hill and down over the railroad tracks to the highway, and we were off for The Landing, with the country sailing by.

2

I guess I should stop and clear up some matters about who I am, actually, what I look like, and what bugs me and that sort of thing, although as far as I am concerned a little of this sort of thing can go a long way, so I'll keep it short. Not too much to tell anyway.

To begin with, I am fifteen years old and my name is Rodney Gerald Blankhard. That's what people call me, Rodney. And I guess that ought to tell you something about me right there. No nickname for me. It is clear that up to now at least I haven't struck any of my contemporaries, north or south, as being an old buddy Rod or a big-wheel R. G. type. Easy mixing is not my strong point. I'm sorry about that, but it's the truth. Also, I am tall for my age. When you are tall you can either slump or stand up straight. I stand up straight. Maybe too straight. Because there is this one wise guy at school that calls me Sir Rodney. He is one of those cute ones that has funny names for everybody. But that's the picture and enough to go on, I would think; I am tall, skinny, generally quiet, and around girls, anyhow, I'm nowhere.

I have this friend, sort of, where I live in White Plains, New York, who is really with it when it comes to girls, or at least he claims he is, and keeps telling me that one of these days some great chemical thing will happen and I will really get turned on and my whole life will start clicking away like an atomic pile or something, and I won't be the same guy, by which he means a drag. Well, I have news for him about being turned on. I stay turned on. I just don't do anything about it.

I'm trying to be honest. Girls drive me half nuts. They don't even have to be sensationally beautiful or have great knockers, as my friend calls them, or, his specialty according to him, low-hung butts. They just have to be alive and walk by. If they smile they're beautiful. If they are shy as well, I am in love. If they have a natural way about them and move easy when they walk, as far as I'm concerned, they've got it.

If this sounds like it is all a matter of biology, that is not how it really seems to me at all, although there is no denying that biology matters, too. Like that is a pretty big difference, all right, the biological one, between a boy and a girl. Just about as big a difference in people, generally speaking, as I have come across yet. But that's about it, and how smart I am when it comes to girls. I read all the time about what the kids today know and do. Not this kid. For instance, a little thing, but an example. One day at school this girl called my name and I turned around and she came running down the walk toward me, moving as natural and easy as you could imagine, and then she stopped in front of me smiling and breathing hard, from the exercise, I guess, and said my name again, a girl I hardly knew except that I knew that she sat two seats over across from me in English. And all she wanted, she said, and it *was* probably all she wanted, was the next day's English assignment. But this could have led to a decent conversation, at least. But not with me it couldn't. Because what I did then, with this pretty girl standing there in front of me still breathing a little hard, which I couldn't help noticing, was what I will always do on a rare occasion like this. What I do is stand up straight and freeze and say something idiotic if I am able to say anything at all. And that's what I did, and that was that with that girl. Except that for the next week I could close my eyes in class any time I wanted to and see the whole thing just as it happened. And sit there and curse myself for a coward and a fool.

So what I have not told my friend about his great theory about how someday I'll get turned on until I am practically a sex fiend is that what I would like to do is to get turned off now and then. Just so that I could be natural with girls and not all eyes and two left feet whenever I get near them, old silent Sir Rodney, standing there with my hands hanging down at my sides like an ape, and with a feeling in the back of my mind that I must be some kind of a nut. It's hell sometimes, and that's the truth.

But that's about the biggest problem I've got, and probably not worth the time I have already given to it. The other problem, and this makes sense at least, is about where I am apt to be living from one day to the next. This has been a problem ever since my mother died when I was thirteen. I get along fine with my father, but half the time he's somewhere down in Latin America or over in Asia or almost anywhere, and while I think I could take care of myself all right when he is away, he says it just wouldn't be right for me to live alone, and I can see his point. But there is no point in going into all of this at any great length, either; but it explains how I spent a summer a year ago on The Hill with my Uncle Charles, and how, miserable and practically disastrous as that summer was, when I had a choice this summer between my Aunt Clara in Mount Vernon and Uncle Charles on The Hill, I thought it over and I couldn't figure what else I could do wrong on The Hill that I hadn't done the year before, so I picked The Hill.

I wouldn't say that knowing Ellen Haywood would be there had nothing to do with it, however silly that may seem, even to me, but that wasn't all of it, either. I mean that what I would have been doing in Mount Vernon all summer would have been pretty much what I had been doing all along in White Plains. Or to put it another way, one city to me is pretty much like another, but The Hill is like no place else that I know. It's mostly nature, I guess, and what I know about nature is nothing at all. So as far as I know, that's the real reason I decided to try it again. Although sometimes, even in the few weeks I have been here, this strikes me as having been a pretty cockeyed reason, at that.

Leaving The Hill, we turned north. I would have sooner turned south, as about thirty or so miles to the south is the Gulf, where there are usually a lot of people on the beach fooling around and nobody notices you much, the way it is with crowds. At The Landing, there is only one house back up

14

from the river where some people named Matthews live, friends of the Haywoods. The time I met them there were only these two old people who had as little to say about anything as any two people I have ever met. For the rest, there is nothing at The Landing that I could remember but this one flat clearing down at the edge of a creek called the Little Star, surrounded by one hundred per cent nature. Personally, I'm more at home with crowds. Trees and shrubbery don't do much for me, although I will say that the way the creek comes twisting down through these woods and the way the clearing opens up right at The Landing, when you come up on it, it's a pretty enough sight in a way. Something you don't expect, anyhow; not so much a place for people, but just a place, all to itself. You get the feeling that it has been just like that forever, although it probably hasn't. On the other hand, natural and perfect as it seems, you find out pretty quick that there is not too much you can do with it, either. Unless you are crazy about fishing, which I'm not, particularly.

Jack is a nut about it, though, although to care about fishing like he does it is surprising how few fish he seems to catch. But then, to Jack, almost everything he does is half a joke. He just enjoys himself.

Sometimes I wish I was more like that myself. Like right at the time, for instance; here we had been heading north all the time on this nice straight macadam highway, the morning still cool enough, the green pine woods and the brown and green fields sliding past us big and slow and open the way you could never see it in a movie or any other way, with now and then a bird singing as we went past and Ellen's long black hair whipping around in the wind beside me, and instead of really enjoying all this I have a polite conversation going on with Ellen, which I have to shout a little to do to be heard above the wind, telling her all about all the crazy places around the world I have managed to listen to with my Star Roamer set. Which seemed to interest her all right, because she kept asking me more about it, as though I was not just a kid with a short-wave set, but kind of an expert on the world itself. As though I had been to all these places. Made me feel a little phony.

Then we turned east off the highway onto a dirt road that got both hilly and bumpy in a hurry, and polite conversation got pretty much impossible under the circumstances, which sometimes included the possibility, it seemed, of one of us getting bounced clean out of the pickup into a ditch. Naturally this was the time that Jack decided to open up his tackle box and untangle all the junk in it and straighten it all out. "Jack," Ellen hollered at him, "you are out of your mind." But Jack just grinned at us and went on holding the tackle box between his knees and bouncing when he had to bounce, with all the stuff in the tackle box bouncing, too, so that at times he looked like some overgrown weirdo trying to play a game of jacks sitting down. Guess it seemed like a challenge to him.

He was still working at it when we got to The Landing, and the tackle box still looked like as big a mess to me as it had looked at the start. But when the truck stopped and Jack saw where we were, he just shut up the box and said, "Well, I'm sure glad that's done," and jumped out of the pickup and started hauling stuff out, while Ellen sat there shaking her head for a while.

Then Ellen and I jumped out, too, and started helping him, first setting up some sawhorses and putting planks across them for a table—these were already there, stored under a hunk of canvas at the back of the clearing—and then Jack and I fixed up the tent his mother and father would use. That was the canvas that Ellen and I had been sitting on, I found out. It wasn't a tent exactly, but a big piece of canvas with mosquito netting sewed to it all around, and which I never could have figured out if it hadn't been for Jack. We stretched it over a rope tied between two trees at the back of the clearing, and tied the corners to other trees, and that was it. You could see clean through it. "That's so they can get a breeze if there is one," Jack said.

Ellen, I noticed, had a tent of her own, a new one that came wrapped in a plastic bag so small that I had thought all along it must be a sleeping bag. But it was Ellen's tent and she put it up herself in no time at all, out at the front of the clearing as close to the creek as she could get it. "Ellen likes to hear the frogs and the creek and all when she sleeps," Jack said, "although it seems to me kind of silly. Especially if what she wants is a good night's sleep." I guess it was about the smallest tent for a grown person to use that I'd ever seen, but I knew better than to start a conversation along those lines with Jack, as he would have thought of something smart to say, one way or another. I had wondered all along about what the sleeping arrangements were going to be, but I hadn't said anything to him about that, either.

And then the food and everything else was out of the back of the pickup and there was nothing left but the canvas that had been over the boxes of food to keep out the dust and a couple of old dusty blankets. Jack still hadn't said anything about where we would be sleeping, and now I really began to wonder about it, because Mr. and Mrs. Haywood had cots and sheets and blankets and pillows in their tent, and Ellen had sheets and a pillow anyhow, but I couldn't see anything left for Jack and me to be comfortable with at all. In fact I didn't see anything left that looked like it could possibly keep us dry if it rained, or, unless we slept in our clothes, that would keep us decent, so to speak. I worried about it for a while, while Jack and his father were over looking at the two boats they had come to repair and trying to decide which one was in the worst shape, and then Ellen came over to me where I was still standing by the pickup. "I hope you are prepared to rough it some," she said, "because if I know Jack he probably hasn't bothered to bring a thing to keep you two boys out of the rain or off the ground tonight but a couple of old blankets." Then she looked in the back of the pickup and saw for herself, and shook her head. "Ma never should have left it up to Jack," she said. "Honest, it's like he thinks he's some kind of animal that can just lie down and sleep on the ground."

"That's all right," I said. "If it's good enough for Jack it's good enough for me. Anyhow, it will be an experience."

"I'm afraid that just being around Jack sometimes can be an experience," Ellen said. "I sure hope you get a decent night's sleep, though."

17

"Well," I said to Ellen to change the subject, "I see the others are already working on the boats so I guess I ought to see if there is some damage I can do there myself. I didn't come along just for the ride, you know."

"I am sure you can be a big help if you want to," Ellen said, "and you must stop running yourself down like that. Everybody has forgot about last summer but you." She was referring to a number of stupid things I had done the summer before when I first came to The Hill, like getting dragged through the lot on my face by a yearling cow I had lassoed and couldn't turn loose, and other things, including last, but not least, smoking in my uncle's barn and probably being the one that set it on fire, although this couldn't be proved one way or the other, as well as it being a wreck of a barn that was about to fall down of its own accord anyway, and not much of a loss, as Mr. Haywood said. None of which Ellen had forgotten, I was sure, but I didn't argue with her, either.

We went over to the boats, and Jack and Mr. and Mrs. Haywood were working on the biggest boat of the two, sanding and scraping away at the blistered paint on the bottom of it and along the sides, sending dust and chips of paint flying up into the air all around them. We stood watching a minute, and it looked simple enough to me, and then Jack said, "If you two get tired of standing, you can drag up a log and sit down. If you don't mind our sweat."

"It is only the hot air that might bother me," I said. "Where is some sandpaper?"

"Rodney and I will do the other boat," Ellen said.

"Better watch that he does not rub a hole right through the bottom," Jack said.

"Ignore him," Ellen said. "He hasn't figured out yet what you meant by that remark about hot air."

"I figured it out," Jack said. "I am just ignoring it."

"That's real sweet," Ellen said, and then we went over to the other boat, which they had moved over out of the way, and got it up, bottom side up, onto some logs we dragged over, and started sanding it. It wasn't in near as bad shape as the other one, and Ellen got on one side and I got on the other and we were able to move right along with it, as well as to talk a little about this and that while we worked. The only thing that began to bother me after a while was that the logs hadn't really lifted the boat up high enough. My back began to hurt, and I got tired of talking to Ellen most of the time without looking at her. I am somewhat taller than Ellen, despite the difference in our ages, but it was a quite a good distance that she had to bend down, too. She kept working right across from me, so that we could talk, I guess. Anyhow, if I moved up or back along the boat, Ellen would move up or back, too. It might have been different with a girl developed along smaller lines, or even just a lazier girl, not sanding so hard all the time, or if Ellen hadn't been wearing one of those baggy fall-away kind of blouses, which as a matter of fact had struck me at first as being kind of shapeless. I'm no prude or silly kid about these certain natural physical characteristics of girls, even when they are more characteristic with some than with others; but this is not a phenomena that has come to bore me to death yet, either. Anyhow, it was clear to me that all Ellen was interested in was sanding the boat, and so I stayed bent down, much as my back got to hurting, watching where I was sanding like a hawk, which Ellen bragged about later to the others, saying that I was the most careful sander she had ever seen. And if it struck her as an odd way to have a conversation, she never mentioned it and neither did I, although toward noon I did make some references to the condition of my back, and Ellen said, "You'll get used to it," meaning one thing, and I said, "I doubt it," meaning another, and Ellen laughed in a way that made me wonder.

We stopped at noon and ate and then rested a bit. I noticed we were all pretty sweaty and sort of stained with the color of the boats we had been working on, Mr. and Mrs. Haywood and Jack looking somewhat ghostly, you might say, and Ellen and I kind of streaked with red. Ellen had a big smear of it across her forehead, and some of her hair was stuck to her cheek. I was thinking how pretty she looked, even so, when she looked and caught me staring at her and laughed and said, just for me to hear, "I guess you and me are a strange pair all right."

No doubt it was mostly just our looks at the time that she was referring to, but the way she laughed, it was hard to tell. This is a new thing I have noticed recently, a certain way of laughing Ellen has sometimes now, as though there is more to the joke than meets the eye, which I am supposed to understand as well as Ellen, but which I am not always so certain about. But Jack had heard her and naturally could not let it pass. "Ha," he said, "that's the truth for sure."

I let it pass. "Well," I said to Ellen, "that's better than being a pair of strangers, I guess." I thought it was a pretty good answer, under the circumstances, with Jack standing there watching us both like he was watching a ping-pong game or something. But all he said this time was, "Ha." I could see I had surprised Ellen considerably, too. To be honest, it had surprised me as well.

So I got up and went down to the creek and glanced at my reflection and saw I was a mess, all right, and then I walked along at the edge of the clearing by the creek, noticing some honeysuckle blooming there, climbing up a post. It seemed a funny place for someone to put in a post and plant some honeysuckle, but there it was. I was wondering about this when Ellen came up beside me and said, "I see you have found the skiff."

I looked around, having no idea what she was talking about. "What skiff?" I said. "All I have found is this honeysuckle."

Then Ellen went over to the edge of the creek and looked down into some tall weeds and grass right next to the water. "If you will look in around the wild honeysuckle on that post you'll find a rope tied to it some place, and at the other end of it, if you'll come here and look, is the skiff I was talking about." I went and stood by Ellen and looked, and finally I saw it, just the front of it with a piece broken out, sticking up in the grass, and the rest of it, with all the paint rotted off it and full of water and hardly floating, in up against the bank.

Then I noticed the rope running back through the grass to the post. It didn't make sense to me. Why tie up a sunk boat? Seemed a little sad even, like whoever had owned it had just gone off and said to hell with it. "See?" Ellen said. "I thought you had discovered it for yourself."

She actually seemed to think it was something, and this confused me, and so I tried to think of something funny to say. "Well," I said, "I certainly hope nobody drowned in the wreck." Ellen didn't even smile, just looked at me puzzled, and I tried again. "A terrible sea disaster," I said, and I heard a grunt this time, and I turned and there was Mr. and Mrs. Haywood standing on the bank behind me. It was Mr. Haywood who had grunted; then Jack came running up.

"Well," Jack said, like he was real happy about it, "I see you have found the skiff."

It was getting monotonous. "Either that or a dead horse," I said. "Let us pull in the rope and see. But in either case, I'm afraid we have found it too late. The most we could do is to bury it." I had thought this would be good for a chuckle or two from someone, but there was not a sound. But I couldn't stop, it seemed. "Naturally," I said, "having been at the bottom of the creek so long it will be too wet to burn." With this last remark it was finally altogether clear to me that for some reason or other I was nowhere near being as smart right then as I had hoped.

Then Mr. Haywood nodded as though he understood. "I guess Rodney has never seen a cypress skiff before, left in the water to keep it tight."

Nobody else seemed to have anything to say right away then, so I said, "No, sir, I guess I haven't. I am not familiar with boats of any sort, to tell the truth, and under water like that, it just looked like a hunk of junk to me. I guess it's your boat?"

I was sure of it by then, particularly the way Jack was looking at me, like I had flipped my lid while he stood there watching. "I built it," Mr. Haywood said.

There was some more silence and then I said, "Oh."

"Twenty years ago," Jack said. "Before you was born."

21

Again there was nobody in any hurry to say anything else, and finally I said, "I thought it looked old, all right."

When I get my foot in my mouth it sometimes seems I will have to blow my head off to get it out. So I decided to see if I could only shut up for a while. Then Jack got down in the weeds and Ellen did, too, and started tugging at the skiff. It seemed the least I could do was help. So not saying anything I got down there with them, and I had hardly got there when I slipped somehow and the next thing I knew I was swimming around in the creek with my clothes on. But then as long as I was in the creek anyhow, I swam up to the back of the boat and tried to push it some, which didn't do any harm at least; and then to my surprise the skiff was up on the bank with all the water dumped out, and I stood there dripping in my wet clothes and admiring it with the rest of them. They all seemed to agree that it had come through the winter just fine. I looked, and I couldn't find any holes in it, either. Just that one little piece missing at one end.

Then they left it to dry out some and went back to sanding, except for Ellen, who stayed with me a while, still looking at the skiff. I had never seen a boat quite like it before. If it had ever been painted, there was no paint left on it now. It was just bare wood, dark and smooth. It was small and neat and came to a point the same on both ends, with one seat in the middle and two small seats near the ends. The name skiff seemed to fit it perfectly, like a description. "I'm sure sorry I made those smart remarks about your father's skiff," I said.

"That's all right," Ellen said, "how could you have known?"

"Well," I said, "I could have waited and found out, I guess," and Ellen couldn't think of any argument for that, and we went back to sanding our boat like the others were doing. I didn't even bother to change out of my wet clothes. Being such a wise guy about Mr. Haywood's skiff had dampened down my pleasure in the day considerably, and being wet as well for a while seemed right enough.

But Ellen went on talking away while we worked as though she hadn't noticed how I had made a fool of myself, and after a time I began to forget it, too. By the time we had finished sanding the red boat I was dry again and Mr. Haywood was already starting to paint on the white one, singing while he worked, which I had never heard him do before, and Jack had worked the skiff back in the creek by himself and was hollering for us to hurry up and go swimming with him. So I got my suit and went one way into the woods and Ellen got hers and went another, and I was back and waiting for her in the boat with Jack when she finally came walking out of the woods and down to the pier in a suit that surprised me more than I hope I let show. The top part of it was practically a sack, or two sacks really, one being made of a kind of net you could see through and under that another sack that you couldn't, and all of it hanging down in about as shapeless a way as I have ever seen it managed with the top of a girl's bathing suit yet. It was something you couldn't help but notice. And the shorts were just as short and tight as the top was baggy, and you would have to notice that, too, if you had eyes at all. Anyhow, when Ellen came walking up, the impression anyone would have to get was that she was mostly a matter of long white legs.

I didn't say a word about it, naturally, but Jack, who hadn't seen the suit before, either, I guess, had so much to say about it that it got embarrassing. He waited until we were out of sight of The Landing, heading for the bridge, then first he told Ellen that she must have forgot to take her new suit out of the package before she put it on, and then he said he supposed it had the advantage that she could seine for shrimp with it, as well as swim in it, or do both at once, even. And then he said something which was none of his business but which I had noticed, too, and that was that it looked to him like she ought to be careful about bending over in it, unless there was more to it than met the eye. It hung off her shoulders about the way the blouse she had been working in did. And this made Ellen as mad as I have ever seen her yet, and I didn't blame her.

"It is none of your silly business," she said, "but naturally there is more to it than meets the eye, and if you were not such a nasty stupid little kid still wet behind the ears you would know that. Or you could at least have some decent manners like Rodney and wait and see."

I was sure Ellen hadn't meant that last part just like it sounded, although at the same time I couldn't think of any other way she might have meant it, either. But for once Jack kept his mouth shut and I looked away and did the same, and Jack kept rowing, and Ellen was quiet, too. And then faint at first I heard her start laughing, and I looked and she was sitting in the end seat hiding her face in her hands and shaking her head from side to side and laughing, and I started laughing a little, too, and she stopped long enough and said, "Rodney, if I said what I think I said I'm sorry," and I laughed out and said, "It's all right, Ellen, you said the truth."

And that set Ellen off even harder, and me, too, and finally Jack gave up and stopped rowing and said, "Well I guess I could have waited along with Rodney at that," and then he just leaned on his oars, with Ellen beating him on the back with her fists as hard as she could, which with her laughing still out of control was not very hard.

Finally Jack started rowing again and we got more or less quiet, but every time Ellen would look at me she would get red a little and then start laughing again, and so would I, and that would start Jack acting foolish again. It's a wonder we ever got to the bridge and had our swim, but we did.

Later, after we had all gone to bed for the night, Ellen in her little toy tent and Jack and me out under the stars on the ground, I thought about it and I was surprised that it hadn't embarrassed me more than it had. It had hardly embarrassed me at all, and this kept me awake awhile thinking about it. I finally realized that Jack, being a wise guy like he had, had actually done me a favor. Because what had been really embarrassing me for some time, ever since I had come back to The Hill, was going around trying to pretend I didn't notice a million or so things about Ellen every time I was with her. And now, as though I had come out and said so, I knew it was understood between Ellen and me that I noticed. Or else what had all our laughing been about?

24

3

I was the last one to get to sleep, I believe, and as far as I could tell, the first one awake the next morning. It was surprising how a smooth stretch of grassy ground could turn out to have had so many lumps in it. When I woke up it was still half dark in the clearing and Jack lay sprawled out beside me still sleeping away like a dog. I don't think he had waked up one time during the night, at least not when I had been awake. It looked like he had just flopped down and stayed where he had dropped. I had to admire him for it. I looked up and there were still some stars in the sky, but only the brightest ones, not the millions I had noticed each time I had waked up before and looked around at where I was. So I figured it was close enough to morning to get up.

As I had slept in my clothes, it was easy enough to do. Even so, I kept as quiet as I could. If the others could sleep, I figured, I should let them. So I went down to the pier in the half-dark and sat there awhile in the quiet, watching the light slowly working down through the tops of the trees across the creek, with a kind of warm mist rising up off the water at the same time, and everything slowly coming into view without a sound but the soft still sound that creek water seems to make when that is all there is to hear. Then a bird sang somewhere off in the woods and then stopped, and I realized I had even beat the birds getting up for once.

I guess I sat there doing nothing for a good half hour or so. There was really nothing else to do. I thought a little about Ellen and the way we had laughed together when she had made that mistake after Jack had made his, and I was not so sure that Jack had done me such a favor in the long run at that. In a quiet morning like it was and with plenty of time to think about it, the way Ellen had laughed then, in fact the way she often laughed since I had come back to The Hill, was something that bothered me the more I sat there with nothing else to think about and thought about it.

Then the birds were really starting to get good and waked up, until it began to sound as though they were having a kind of singing contest among themselves, even those that couldn't sing to amount to much chiming in with their special one- or two-note deals, over and over, which I suppose sounded nice enough to them. Down the creek a ways there was one bird—I would guess it was a water bird of some kind, because I could not remember having heard a bird like this around The Hill —and when he sang the notes had a kind of hollow sound or softened sound, the way things will sound around water. It was like it was half held back, or as though he used a mute. Yet it was clear despite that, and quick and climbing, and then it ended on a kind of half-note, every time, as though he stopped before he really had to. Silly as it sounds, it made me think of the way Ellen sometimes laughs, half held back and kind of mysterious, and an aggravation in a way. Anyhow, I noticed this song more than the others and got so I kept waiting for it, thinking about Ellen and me and getting more aggravated about it all the while.

In the early morning when you're alone it is sometimes hard to kid yourself about things, and I guess that was what was bothering me. The truth was, I realized, that since I had come back to The Hill this time, Ellen was insisting more and more on not treating me like she had before, even though that was still pretty much the way I wanted it, with Ellen beautiful and sweet as ever, and me still two years younger, polite as hell, and safe. That was the truth of it, although why that should get me aggravated with a certain pretty bird song was something else again, and not like me at all. As far as I am concerned, birds are birds.

And to be honest and realistic about it, that bird song didn't actually sound like Ellen's way of laughing any more than it sounded like a fire truck. It was just that I couldn't get the whole matter off my mind. On the one hand it seemed I

26

wanted Ellen to take more notice of me, more as an equal, so to speak, and on the other hand it seemed I wasn't so anxious about this after all. And I figured out finally, with no help from the birds, that Ellen probably guessed all this and it was this, sometimes, that made her laugh the way she did. And thinking about it, I realized that there were other things, too, now that I brought them to my attention. The way sometimes I would kid with her as I never would have dared to do before, and the way sometimes when we were out exploring around The Hill in the evenings she would do a little thing like take my hand for a minute, at night, when the path was not plain, as though I would know the way. Like I was obviously not altogether a kid any more; not to her anyhow. And a couple of times when my hair had been messed up she had threatened to get a comb and comb it herself, though naturally she had never done this yet. But then some little thing along this line would come up and Ellen would say something intentional or I would say something by accident but either way it might have some meaning that could be looked at in more ways than one, and then Ellen would wait and when it flustered me, as it usually did, she would laugh.

Not that it is so awful to be laughed at in such a way; it's nice even. There is a friendliness to it that is unmistakable, and she would sometimes put her hand on my arm at such a time as though to say I must not let my feelings be hurt or stay flustered, and I wouldn't. But all of this, nice enough in its way, was not exactly the way I had figured things would be, and this, when I got right down to it and would admit it to myself, which I finally did, hardly hearing the birds sing at all, by that time, was what had come to bug me more than I wanted to say. Jack's stupid fresh remark to his own sister, and then Ellen's remark about me, which certainly hadn't been intended quite like it sounded, this in a way had brought something out in the open between Ellen and me, and while it seemed almost a kind of relief, at least to her, and to me, too, at the time—the way we had laughed, especially—still I had to admit, thinking it over, that things had changed more than I really wanted them changed. The truth was, it kind of took the solid ground out from under me, and left me not only still turned on but sort of turned loose as well, with nothing certain any more except that like it or not there was nothing that could automatically stop me from *really* falling in love with Ellen now, and probably making a fool of myself altogether.

I sure hadn't planned it this way. If I had planned anything in the back of my mind it was only to have it be the way it had been the summer before, with me going around eating my heart out for Ellen and being more polite to her than anything she could have possibly been used to, with this being because of the difference in our ages and being the only way I could give her a good hint about how I felt about her without making a fool of myself in a way you could point your finger at and say, You poor fool, you. To me, come to think of it, it had looked pretty foolproof at that.

But now I knew the truth. With the little special laugh of hers, Ellen had changed all that. And for a while, sitting there thinking about it, it almost made me mad. It didn't seem quite fair somehow. I'd been willing to love and to lose, as they say, without even trying, however ridiculous it might seem; seemed to me that that should have been enough. I shouldn't have had to worry about it, too. And what made me madder all the time was the idea that kept getting clear to me, that it wasn't Ellen's fault at all, but my own. No matter how polite you are about it, it finally seemed to me, if you go out of your way to show a girl that you really like her, why shouldn't she figure that you really mean it?

And what I didn't know was, how much *did* I really mean it?

I looked over toward the tent where Ellen was sleeping, surprised that all along she had been this close and I hadn't turned and noticed it. Her pillow was pushed half out of the tent, and her long black hair was spread all over it. The way the tent was set up, facing the creek, that was all I could see. I looked around and no one else was awake that I could tell, even though it was altogether daylight now; then I looked back at the tent, and when I did Ellen had turned and was awake and looking at me, and she smiled a sleepy, friendly

28

kind of smile I had naturally never seen her smile before, and then she put her face back into the pillow, and went back to sleep, I guess.

I looked back out at the creek for a time not knowing what to think or even what I had spent the morning thinking, just altogether confused and somehow half happy and half miserable at the same time, if that's possible; and then I thought to myself, the hell with this, I've been sitting here long enough as it is, and I got up and without glancing at Ellen's tent I went back to the edge of the clearing and woke up Jack.

It wasn't so easy to do; I had to shake him until his head shook. How he could sleep so sound on ground that hard and in daylight as well I could not imagine. And even then he was not happy about being waked.

"Let's take the skiff and go exploring down the creek," I said.

"I first explored that creek some years ago," Jack said, "but I have never dreamed of flying an airplane before, which you just ruined for me by waking me up. I was the pilot. I think we was lost. The only one that stayed calm was me. But take the skiff yourself if you want. There is only the red boat to paint and then we are through, and I imagine we can manage it without you this one time. Now I would like to go back to sleep and see if I can get started up with that dream again; I hate to leave all those passengers in such danger." Then he laughed, at himself, I guess, because I hadn't said a word, and lay back down to sleep if he could.

Well, I thought, I would just as soon go without him anyhow. I had never been farther down the Little Star Creek than a few bends below The Landing, and with Jack along it would not be a matter of exploring so much as a matter of a guided tour, with such interesting landmarks pointed out as where he almost caught a ten-pound catfish once, or shot at a ten-foot water moccasin and missed, or where somebody drowned, through no fault of his. Mostly, I wanted to get away from The Landing for a while. Mostly from Ellen. Or anyhow, just to be alone, and maybe get my mind off my own nature and that of girls and see for myself if there was anything going on of interest in just plain old nature itself, new and unknown to me as it was, here as elsewhere.

I went back into the woods where I had hung my swimming trunks out to dry on a limb. Even though they were still practically dripping, I changed into them, in case I wanted a morning swim, and went back to the clearing where everyone was still sleeping or still trying to, and got into the skiff, and somehow not making it look nearly as easy as it should have looked, I rowed on down the creek and out of sight of The Landing, leaving Jack dreaming of staying calm while his sensible passengers screamed in panic, if that was the case, and Ellen still sleeping, or at least with her black hair still spread out around on her pillow the careless way I had seen it last, when she had smiled at me and then gone back to sleep, as though there was nothing unusual or to be worried about, about this or anything else in the world.

I was glad when The Landing was out of sight and I knew I was on my own for a while. Right away, it seemed, I got the knack of rowing worked out and had no more trouble to speak of with it. The skiff, once I got used to it and the quick way it moved along and could be turned so easy, seemed about as right for me as any kind of boat that had to be rowed could be. I had done some rowing before, but usually in boats that would have been better off sunk, in my opinion, tubs that not even an expert could row without feeling clumsy. The kind of rowboats they rent out at lakes and public parks, big enough for the whole family and a dog or two as well. You can't really row any place in such boats, you just float around and beat at the water and let it go at that. At least that was my experience with rowing, and Mr. Haywood's old cypress skiff was certainly a nice surprise to me. Made me feel like I had a natural right to be rowing down Little Star Creek at that, stranger to it or not. Seemed to me, at least, that for a while there I just shot along, winding and narrow as the creek was.

Then I slowed down. There was no point in speed particularly, I figured; one part of the creek was as new to me as another, with all of it, so far, looking more or less the same. There hadn't been another single clearing on either side since

I had left The Landing, not a house or a sign of people anywhere. Just the creek, deep and clear and black-looking, with still some streaks of mist rising up off it here and there, a river really, if you think of a creek as being something more or less along the line of a brook, but, by whatever name, winding and curving along so easy and slow it hardly seemed to be moving at all, with woods as thick and tangled as jungles almost, coming right up to the water's edge on either side, like two big walls. I had never been out alone on such a creek before in my life. I wouldn't say it was scary exactly, but you could say it was strange, to say the least. The quietness of it, especially.

Then I passed a little brook of some kind running into the creek, and I thought about exploring it, but then I decided I would stay with the Little Star to avoid any confusion about where I was or how to get back again later. Right past the place where I had seen the little brook, the creek started around the biggest and longest bend I had come across yet, widening out at the same time in a way that surprised me, until it must have been a good block or so wide, and still curving away. I stayed close to the side I was already nearest to, and after a while I noticed that the trees were thinning out some along the shore, and then I came to a place where there was a sandy beach ahead of me, plain to see, and when I got to it the water was shallow and sandy along the bottom as well, and there was even enough of a clearing in the trees so that I could have landed and explored it some if I had wanted to. But I wanted to get on around the bend, which seemed as though it had no end to it, and I had found out already that there is something about going down a strange river that once you start into a bend you have a strong wish to see what is around at the other end. So I kept on, and finally the bend came to an end, and started another big bend, back the other way. And right there was another little brook, bigger than the first one I had seen; and for no good reason I decided to explore it.

I hadn't gone any distance at all when I worked my way around a little bend and to my confusion out in front of me was another creek every bit as big if not bigger than the Little Star. Jack hadn't mentioned another such creek, and this puzzled me, but then I thought, well I'll try it for a ways and see where it goes. After all, exploring was what I had set out to do. So I explored it a ways, and then started around another big bend, which kept going on and on and getting wider, and I got more and more suspicious that maybe I hadn't discovered anything so new at that; and when I came to the sandy beach again I stopped and got out and feeling pretty foolish I said for the birds to hear, "I claim this crazy island in the name of Rodney Gerald Blankhard, Sir Nut, himself." And it's the truth, right then a big crow flew by high up over my head and went caw, caw, caw, three times. "Drop dead, you wise guy," I said to him, and then I got back in the skiff and went on down the stream, still feeling pretty foolish for a while for thinking I was discovering a river when all I had been doing was rowing all around an island that I hadn't had sense enough to know was an island. I guess it was the deep woods on both sides that confused me about it; they had made everything look pretty much the same. Anyhow, details in nature have to be pretty obvious for me, like here is a woods, there is a field, or I am apt to miss them altogether.

It wasn't more than a few bends farther down, with the creek widening out regular by this time, that I came to the first sure sign of civilization I had come upon yet. It wasn't much, just a barbed wire fence running down the side of a cleared field right down to the water's edge, where there was a post stuck up with a sign on it that said, PRIVATE, KEEP OUT. So I knew there must be people somewhere around. I must admit that for some reason it made me feel somehow relieved.

I have said it was a cleared field, but what it really was was just a large clearing. What the fence was for I couldn't figure out, as I saw no cattle or horses or any signs that they might have been there and had gone, so what the fence was supposed to keep either in or out was a mystery. There weren't even any boats there, nothing at all. Still, the sign was clear enough in what it said, and though I would have liked to stop and explore a little there, I kept going. As far as I am concerned, private property is private property, wherever you find it.

But it wasn't much longer until I came to my next sign of civilization, though if I hadn't been going slow and trying to observe my surroundings I might have missed it at that. It was just a path. It was at a place where it looked like there might have been a clearing once, but it had been left neglected and grown up again to grass and bushes. It had a kind of abandoned look about it even, like an empty lot with trash in it, or a lonely look, anyhow, an empty clearing in the woods at the edge of the river, of no use to anyone. But then I saw the path, plain to see once I had seen it, coming down through the tall grass as far back up it as I could see and coming right down to the edge of the river, and, naturally, stopping there. I looked, and there wasn't any sign around saying keep off, but I knew that the path meant people, for sure, so after thinking about it I took a chance that they wouldn't mind if I explored a little and I pulled the skiff up enough on the bank to hold it from drifting off, and having nothing better to do in the way of exploring I started following the path back up away from the river.

The ground rose up fairly steep for a ways, and I went straight up it following the path; then it ran more or less level for a time, with the path beginning to curve about some here and there even when it seemed to me that some of the clumps of weeds and little low bushes it went curving around could have just as easily been stepped over. Well, I thought, maybe the path has been made by old people or by kids. One thing for sure, I figured, it's a path, and a path has got to lead someplace.

So I kept following it, and it twisted about more and more in a way that didn't seem reasonable to me at all, but I figured that if the people that made it could put up with it so could I. Then it turned and went down a long slope, going more or less straight again for a change, and I could see it was leading on into a pretty big kind of woods that looked more and more tangled the closer I got to it. If there was a house anywhere

33

back in there it stayed well hidden from my sight by the trees. Then the grass thinned out and gave way to only bushes and shrubs and things of that sort, and the path had to be watched carefully or I could see I might lose it. And I was bent down watching where I was going and staying right on the path when the next thing I knew I had been led right up against a thicket of some kind, higher than my head and solid almost as a wall, with no way for a man to get through it at all. And the path went right on into it.

I stood and looked down at the path going on into the thicket and there was no mistaking it, that was where it went. There was a time then, not long, really, I suppose, but it certainly seemed long enough, when I just stood there looking down, hardly knowing what to think, hearing some bees or some insects of some kind humming around in the still air, and feeling the sun shining down bright on my bare back, feeling like some kind of stupid giant. Then I stayed quiet and got down on my knees and sighted along the ground where the path disappeared into the thicket, and I could see where it went on for a ways, like a tunnel, and then twisted and turned and curved out of sight. I knew by this time that it had been an animal path I followed, and not a big animal, at that. I guess you could say that in a quiet sort of way I was amazed.

And then I got up and looked around, and the sky seemed about ten times bigger than it had ever seemed before, and the sun brighter and the trees taller, and I, myself, seemed to have changed, as though I had never really noticed myself before, or at least not in this way, as alive in the woods and a part of it all, like anything else that lives. It was a strange feeling.

Then I got a little more reasonable about it and started wondering what kind of animal it was that made such a path, and I got down again and searched around in the path and finally came up with one little hair of some kind left hanging on a twig, pretty much like a dog's hair, about an inch or so long and grey-colored. It didn't give me too much of a clue. Just about any small animal I could think of could have a grey-colored hair somewhere on it, whether a rabbit, squirrel,

34

raccoon or even a fox. Squirrels seemed the least likely to me to have made such a path, mostly because they are known to live in trees, so I ruled out squirrels. But for the rest, it could have been anything. I had looked for animal tracks, but the ground was dry and slick as cement where the path was down to bare dirt, and anyhow if I had seen a dozen different tracks clear I wouldn't have been able to tell one from the other.

But by this time my curiosity had been aroused, and I thought, well, it is still a path, even if one for some animal and not for people, but a path of any sort still has got to lead to someplace. I figured that if I could go around the thicket I might see where the path came out of it on the other side, if it did come out, then I could follow it until it finally led to wherever it was that whatever it was lived. It seemed worth a try anyhow.

So I started working my way around the thicket, staying as close to it as I could, and lucky for me it turned out not to be too big a thicket, and soon I was on the other side of it, with the woods just beyond. I looked for the path again, at first with no luck, and I was about to give up on it when I found it, leading out of the thicket on this side as clear as it had led into it on the other. The way this pleased me, you would have thought I had just solved a murder or something. Once I had found the path again, it was easy enough to follow it on over and into the woods, but there in the pine straw and leaves on the ground it wasn't nearly as clear. But it could still be followed, and for a ways more I followed it, and then, just as if it had been done to throw anyone following it off the track, the path split up and became first two paths and then a whole bunch of them, with all of them getting fainter until one by one I lost them all and had to give up on it.

I sat down on a log and rested and thought about it, and what it amounted to, I decided, was that I had been outwitted by some unknown animal about the size of a cat with at least some grey hair on it. That was as close as I could come to the truth of it. But what the meaning was of the path leading to no place, of it just breaking up into a bunch of paths and then plain disappearing, this bugged me. But then heading back to the river and the skiff, going by the thicket again, it came to me. Why would any animal bother to make a path through a thicket that big when he would go out of his way to go around even a couple of small bushes? Because that was where he lived; in the thicket. And then the whole thing made sense to me, disappearing paths and all. The paths didn't disappear where I had thought they did; that was where they *started,* and where they led to, naturally, was the thicket and home. Home for what I still didn't know, but I was almost as satisfied as if I did.

As animals go, it seemed to me I hadn't proved to be such a dumb one finally myself. As for the other animal, whatever it was, I hoped it wouldn't notice or mind the way I had spent so much time tramping up and down on his own little path. At least I had stayed out of his thicket, and if I had really wanted to, I think I could have crawled on in there, though no doubt the branches would have scratched me up considerably.

And I was feeling pretty good about the whole thing when I got back to the creek, even though it had taken more time than I had meant it to, and even though it didn't strike me as something I could very well explain or brag about to Jack or Ellen when I got back to The Landing. And I guess I stood on the bank of the creek for a good sixty seconds or so, right where the path starts up from it and right where I had left the skiff, before I could really get it through my head that the skiff was gone.

4

It was an awful feeling, standing there in that bright sun looking out at the creek and seeing it clear and empty both ways for as far as I could see, and Mr. Haywood's skiff absolutely gone, nowhere in sight, vanished, like it had gone up in thin air. I had never really thought about that expression much, gone up in thin air, but if you have ever stood like I did then, looking around on the ground where you had left it and then up and down a river as far as you could see and finally looking up in the air even, up in the treetops and beyond, wondering what has happened to your lost skiff, then you can appreciate such an expression. That's about the way you feel. Like it has gone up in thin air, or anyway, however impossible it seems, it is gone and that's that.

It was an awful feeling, and the longer I stood there the worse it got. For a while I think I could have cried. It wasn't that I was scared or worried about getting back to The Landing, although I could see that was going to be a problem worth thinking about. It was that it was Mr. Haywood's skiff, and that it was gone and it was nobody's fault but mine. And it was not just any skiff, but a wonderful, amazing little skiff that he had built himself, and which Jack had claimed would practically last forever. Well, not now, it won't, I thought, not up at The Landing, anyhow, or where Mr. Haywood will know about it.

It had plainly been stolen. Someone passing by had known what a worthless-looking old skiff like that was really worth and had simply tied it behind their own boat and sneaked on down the creek with it. And if I had tied it to a tree, or if I hadn't of gone off and just left it, looking like it might have drifted there, even, then most likely it would still be right where I had left it instead of gone. And whether somebody had stolen it or had just thought they had found it didn't matter too much. The thing was that it was gone, and for all I knew, gone forever. For a while it made me just about half sick, the plain straight shock of it. If there had been some others around and we had all talked about it, then it might have been different. But all there was was the creek and this little scrubby clearing and the sky and the quiet and no skiff. And that was the way I had to face it finally, and decide about what I had to do next.

I decided to swim back up to The Landing. It seemed the only sensible thing to do. The one thing I do well, along with basketball, is swim. I am not always happy about some of the creatures you can find yourself swimming with in an Alabama river, such as gars and alligators and snakes of all kinds, but they will generally mind their business, I'm told, if you mind yours, and anyhow my experience is that you hear more about these creatures than you actually see them. Once I did see an alligator in a swimming hole over in back of The Hill, and while I wasn't swimming in it at the time, I had got out of it not more than five minutes before I did see it, and probably would have got out a good deal sooner if I had known for sure it was there. That was what the hole was called, the 'gator hole. But water itself holds no fear for me.

It would be a long swim, a couple of miles, at least, but I knew I could rest along the way if I had to. But it was either swim or wait to be missed and looked for and found, and that seemed too much of a humiliation. Having lost the skiff was bad enough. And if I swam back, I figured, it might sort of prove to them that I cared, because nobody would swim that far just to get back home and say they had lost a skiff unless they felt about as sorry about it as a person could feel.

Looking at it this way made me feel a little better, so I looked up at the sky and figured it must be right about noon, and then I slipped into the creek and started swimming. I was sure glad I had worn my trunks.

The day had heated up to such a point that at first the water was a welcome relief, and I swam right along, as though

I was taking a dip in the pool at the Y, but soon enough I realized that this was no sensible way to start out on a two mile swim up a river, going against the current at that, and I slowed down to a more reasonable speed. Coming down in the skiff, I had noticed how the woods on either side seemed to glide right by, but I could soon see that going back I would be getting a different look at them. One tree at a time, so to speak.

It was slow going. But pretty soon I reached the clearing with the fence and the sign saying private, and because I remembered that it was a good ways up to the island where the next clearing was, I ignored the sign and swam in and went ashore and sat in the clearing and rested for a time. I could have used some shade, but there wasn't any, so as soon as I noticed I was starting to sweat some from the sun I decided I could rest better in the creek if I had to, and I started back up it, going slow and easy and not bothering to look at the shore too much to see how much distance I was making. It was too discouraging.

After a while it was clear that easy as I was taking it I was still tiring some, so I started loafing along on my back quite a bit. This arrangement would have been fine except that I was looking straight up into the sun most of the time, which meant I had to go swimming along on my back with my eyes closed. And while I probably couldn't have done a thing about it if I had seen a snake or an alligator or gar swimming along with me, I sure didn't like the idea of not being able even to see it. It just didn't seem natural to swim in a river such as this as though it were nothing but a lot of water. Also, up to then, hopeless as it seemed, I had been keeping my eye out for Mr. Haywood's skiff, just in case whoever had taken it might have later thought better of it and turned it loose or put it ashore somewhere. But to get rested, some of the time that was the way I had to do it, with my eyes closed, an easy prey if it should come to that for just about anything.

I tried not to think about this, but sometimes I couldn't help it. Finally it happened that some floating pine straw, a whole bunch of it, green, I later discovered, although I had thought green wood was supposed to sink, came floating along with the current and I was on my back resting with my eyes closed and without warning it caught up right alongside of my ear. I didn't holler or anything, but I believe that for a second there I was almost clear of the water. I know for certain anyhow that I hit my own ear so hard that I had a ringing in it long after the commotion had all died down. And until I beat that prickly bunch of pine needles off the back of my neck where they had lodged and saw that I had not been attacked after all, there was quite a commotion all right.

After that I decided that sink or swim I was through with resting on my back for the rest of the trip. And by this time, too, I had noticed that I had got my second wind, and I settled down to some serious swimming and moved along steady for maybe another half an hour or so. Judging from the way the sun had moved in the sky from where I had spotted it when I first started back, I figured I had been swimming for an hour and a half or so by the time I reached the island and could crawl up on that nice sandy beach and get a decent rest.

I guess I sat and rested, in the shade this time, for fifteen minutes or more. It wasn't much farther up to The Landing, and as a point of pride I didn't want to get there not only minus Mr. Haywood's skiff but altogether out of breath and looking half drowned. I don't mind having someone feel sorry for me if there is something to feel sorry about, but not when I have been wrong. And sitting there resting and thinking about Mr. Haywood's skiff I knew how wrong I had been. The least I could have done was to have tied it to a tree; then whoever took it would have clearly been a thief and the fault would hardly have been mine. But the way I had just dragged it up a bit on the shore and walked off and left it there, a person could have come by and honestly believed it had just drifted down the river and got stuck there. I would have thought so myself, if it had of been me. And I knew I would have to tell Mr. Haywood just how it happened and take the blame that would be due. It's not that I am a Boy Scout in a situation such as this, but that I have found out with experience that somehow I cannot tell a real lie and get away with it.

I had already made up my mind to tell the truth before, but sitting there resting I thought it all through again. Maybe I did it just to kill some time. Now that I was almost at The Landing, I began to start feeling pretty much the same way I had felt when I first found the skiff gone, a kind of sick feeling. I believe I felt worse about losing Mr. Haywood's skiff than I felt last summer at the time it was pretty much decided that my smoking in my uncle's barn had been the cause of its being burned to the ground. In the end, in that case, I gave up smoking anyhow; but I couldn't see one thing in the world I could do about the stolen skiff, except maybe get another skiff, if anybody would trust me with it, and go looking for the one I lost. I could make such an offer anyhow, and see what happened.

The more I thought about it the more it seemed the best idea I had had yet and a thing I would have to do, even if I had to build my own skiff first or steal one myself just to have one to go looking for Mr. Haywood's in. After all, I figured, nobody would steal a skiff and take it home and set it out in their back yard for a birdbath or something; they would use it to row around in, and if I looked long enough up and down the creek or wherever there was water I would sooner or later come across it. I doubted if there was another skiff quite like it, anywhere, especially with that little piece missing out of one end of it.

I made up my mind about it, right then and there; and if such things were still possible and I had known how to do it I would have made a solemn vow to that effect. As it was, I just made a promise to myself that I would find Mr. Haywood's skiff for him again if it was the last thing I was ever to do. So feeling fairly human again, I got back into the creek and started swimming away on the last stretch back to The Landing.

I expected to make it without any strain, but somehow or other in the time I had sat resting and thinking on the island

41

it seemed as though the current had increased to about twice as fast as it had been before. I couldn't account for it and didn't really believe it was so at first, but pretty soon there was no doubt about it in my mind. There was a current going against me now that was an altogether different thing and nothing to fool around with, and I knew I was in for a real swim all right before I would make it to The Landing. So I forgot about the skiff and the scenery and everything else and just settled down to swimming.

I guess it wasn't more than a half a mile from the island to the clearing, but it was the longest half a mile I ever tackled, and when I finally got there I was swimming on my back again, altogether winded and closer to being half drowned than I wanted to admit. I guess they weren't looking for me to show up finally swimming but were watching only for the skiff; anyhow, when I got near they were all busy loading stuff in the truck at the back of the clearing, and once they gave a loud blast on the horn, for me, I guess, but by that time I was in near the pier and out of their sight. I had just got even with the pier and was wondering if I had the strength to pull myself out when I heard a little scream, sort of, and I turned my head as best I could and there was Mrs. Haywood standing there with a bucket in her hand staring at me like I was a ghost. Then she dropped the bucket and hollered out, "It's Rodney," and the next thing I knew they were all lined up on the pier staring down at me, where I was floating on my back trying to pretend I wasn't tired and so not even taking ahold of the pier yet, their heads lined up against the sky with every one of them looking more surprised and serious than if I had floated in there a corpse. I could see Mrs. Haywood must have been worried about me because she started hollering for Jack and Ellen to help me out and couldn't they see I was already half drowned and then she started to cry and it got quiet for a minute and I said, "I am all right, Mrs. Haywood, I am just resting."

And then Mr. Haywood said, "What happened, boy?" and they waited, because I guess that was the question on all their minds and it got quiet again and I said, "I'm sorry, Mr. Haywood, but somebody either stole your skiff or thought they found it, but I will find it myself again if it is the last thing I do."

"Oh, you poor boy you," Mrs. Haywood said and started crying again, which made me feel awful, and I turned over and put both hands on the pier, and Jack grabbed one hand and Ellen the other and they started dragging me out. And I couldn't believe it but even at a time like that I noticed the way the top of Ellen's bathing suit fell away and how perfectly smooth and rounded and how much of her there really was, in just the one sight I had, looking up, before I shut my eyes. Then I was standing there on the pier, suddenly dizzy and not even sure why, with Ellen holding her arm around me and holding me up close, and everybody asking me a million questions at once, until finally not knowing what else to do but not wanting to stand there any more like some poor kid being comforted by his mother, I pulled away from Ellen and turned to Jack and said, "Thank you, Jack," and reached out and took his hand and shook it as though he had saved my life.

It took him somewhat by surprise, but I could see it pleased him, too.

5

The trip back in the pickup from The Landing to The Hill was about as educational and as miserable a trip as I've ever had. I would have just as soon been up in an airplane being taught how to fly. It was Jack who took the trouble to set me straight on all the things I had done wrong and figured wrong through the day, although Ellen was some help to him along these lines, too. And Jack wasn't even being the kind of wise guy about it that you would have expected. Seemed clear that he just really believed that no one should be allowed to stay as dumb about things as I was.

We no sooner got started back than he started in. "What your trouble is, Rodney," he said, as though he had been thinking it over now for some time, "is ignorance."

"Now, Jack," Ellen said, "you know as well as I do that it's nothing but inexperience." They argued this a little between them but I didn't care enough to take sides. As far as I was concerned they both were right.

To begin with, all of them, Mr. and Mrs. Haywood, too, did not believe that the skiff had been stolen at all. I had told them the whole thing, exactly as it happened. What they believed was that the tide had come in and floated it free and it had drifted off. Maybe then, they figured—they were mostly being nice about it, I think—someone might have seen it drifting along and taken it in tow. What made them pretty certain about their tide theory about how the skiff got lost was what they all had noticed about the tides themselves during the day and which I could not deny. I hadn't noticed or known until then that a river like Little Star Creek even had tides.

I said so to Jack and Ellen as soon as they finished their

44

argument about my inexperience and ignorance. "I'll take your word for it," Jack said, "even though that seems to me a hard thing not to notice. But if you had got down from Little Star Creek onto Big Star Creek and kept going you would have ended up in Mobile Bay and from there if you wanted to you could have went on to the ocean. Which is where the tides come from."

"All the rivers around here are tidal rivers," Ellen said, "and they rise and fall right along with the regular tides."

"All the way up to their source," Jack said, "where the water can be sweet enough to drink, with not even a hint of salt. Still they rise and fall. They have got no way to avoid it. Further down, near their mouths, they become brackish and should not be drunk, of course, although you would probably figure that out for yourself with a try or two." Jack was being a regular schoolteacher about it, but for once I figured he knew pretty much what he was talking about. More than I did, anyhow. "You don't know how lucky you was," he said, shaking his head in wonder, "swimming back with an incoming tide behind you, even though it was about to turn, and not even knowing the help you was getting. Because when a tide is going out, depending on a lot of other things of course, it can sometimes really go out with a rush."

"That was what happened," Ellen said, "on the last part of your swim from the island to The Landing. The tide had turned and started out."

"It was pure luck you made it back alive," Jack said.

"I guess I should feel lucky all right," I said, "but for some reason or other I don't. I doubt anyhow that later I will be apt to look back at this as one of my most lucky days."

Jack started to argue with me about this a little, but Ellen broke in and mentioned to him I was still a mighty strong swimmer in any event, while Jack himself most likely couldn't have done what I had done even with the best tide going and a good strong wind to help him out. "I would have better sense than to try such a thing," Jack said, "and I also wouldn't have went and lost the skiff." I knew he was right in both cases and we were all quiet for a while and then Jack went back

45

into it. "If it *had* of been me and I had forgot all I ever knew and had gone off following a game trail into the woods leaving the boat there to be carried off by the tide like it was, and if I had come back to find myself marooned through my foolishness and with no transportation, still the furthest I would have swum would have been to that clearing you mentioned with the PRIVATE, KEEP OFF sign and the fence. Because while a game trail may sometimes lead you to water, it can just as often get you lost, but a fence, any fence that's kept up at all, if you follow it long enough it just naturally has to lead you to people." This seemed true enough, though it had not occurred to me, but Jack was not finished with it yet, so I said nothing. "If you had followed that particular fence for less than a mile, where it would have took you, if you took all the turns it takes, was to Stacey's old unused chicken sheds, and from there you could have seen the new ones and even the house itself. Or if not, by this time the dogs most likely would have found you, and old man Stacey or his boy would have thought nothing of driving you back to The Landing. So you see, the way you done it, you could have got drowned for nothing, while if you had done it my way, the most you could have got was dog bit."

I could have pointed out to him that the way it actually worked out I didn't get drowned or dog bit either one, but I did not have the heart for it and anyhow I knew that he was right, even so. So what I finally said was, "Well, I can see the things I did wrong, but that's in the past, and what worries me now is the matter of finding your father's skiff, which I lost." I had wanted to stay on at The Landing and start looking for it as soon as either of the painted boats had got dry enough to be put in the water, but Mr. Haywood had not appeared to think that was such a hot idea. He said no, anyhow. I guess he figured I'd done enough damage already and did not wish to take the risk of more, although he claimed he wasn't really worried about the skiff one way or another or whether it was ever found again or not. Along with Mrs. Haywood he seemed mostly relieved that I hadn't drowned myself.

Jack seemed to be thinking about what I had said, and

finally he said, "Well, I guess I could take some time off and show you where to look, if we can work it out with Pa." It wouldn't have been right to say so right then, but Jack's help in the matter was somehow the last thing I wanted.

"I would look for it up and down the creek," I said. "Where else? All I would need is a boat and a pair of oars."

"And a strong back," Jack said, "if you mean to row. You have never been all the way down it yet; that's a long old creek. My plan would be to use Pa's motor if he would let us. We could do it in half a day, if the speed didn't bother you."

"I would rather row," I said, "however long a creek it is. Down one side and back the other, not missing an inch. That would be my plan."

"It would take several days and give you some blisters on your hands," Jack said. "But it might be fun at that. We could live by catching fish."

"Then both of you would starve," Ellen said, and then before Jack could give her an argument, she turned to me. "You must not be too worried about looking for Pa's skiff right away. If you really mean to take the time to look for it, in the way you say, then you will need more of a plan than just a boat and oars."

I hadn't realized it would be such an undertaking as Jack had suggested, taking several days, but the way I felt about it I would have taken a month at it if I had to. "All right," I said, "I will take some time and work up a plan and figure out what stuff I have to take. I will do it right, if that is what is worrying anybody, and if the skiff can be found I will find it."

I had sounded a little like I was making a speech, so I shut up for a time. I knew that both of them meant well by their advice, but I was not in a mood for it. I had lost their father's skiff, and the first chance I got I meant to do what I could to try and find it, and for the rest I would have been willing to let the matter drop for a time.

So Jack changed the subject by going back over all the things I did wrong the summer before, naming them off one by one and somehow managing to find something he had thought was humorous or at least interesting about each of them. It even got the two of them laughing a little now and then, but if they expected me to laugh with them I was not in the mood for that, either. And then we were home and the pickup bounced over the cattle guard and came to a stop and Jack surprised me by giving me a big slap on the back. "Rodney," he said, "I am sure glad you come back to The Hill again. Maybe you don't never mean to do it, but you liven things up some every time."

I couldn't think of a thing to say to that, so I helped him unload the truck and then I got my stuff and went on across the road to my uncle's. I didn't even have the heart to thank the Haywoods for taking me along; somehow, it wouldn't have seemed right. I figured they would understand.

It was late afternoon when we got back, and though it seemed like a strange time to do it, the first thing I did was take a bath and change my clothes and comb my hair. It didn't help much. Aunt Vera could see that something was wrong, I guess, because she kept asking me if I had enjoyed myself and so on until finally I told her and Uncle Charles that I had lost Mr. Haywood's old cypress skiff. My Uncle Charles is a retired banker who fools around now at farming, and he takes all money matters pretty seriously, from his past experience, I guess. Anyhow, right away he wanted to know what the skiff was worth, and when I said you couldn't put a dollars-and-cents worth on such a skiff, he seemed not to understand. "Well," he said, "I will talk to Mr. Haywood and I imagine he can put a monetary value on it quick enough, and then of course we will have to pay him what he says it's worth. Are you sure it was altogether your fault? There is such a thing, you know, as a true accident or, if you will, an act of God for which you could not be held to account." My uncle talks like that.

"It was no act of God," I said. "It was ignorance. But you won't have to pay Mr. Haywood for it, because I'm going to go back to the creek and find it again for him."

"I suppose that is a possibility," Uncle Charles said. "It

may have been found by some honest person at that; there are still some, I am told, among the rural poor who believe it wrong to lie or steal. Perhaps we should wait upon the outcome of your search before mentioning the matter of recompense to Mr. Haywood. I am sure he would rather have his skiff back than the few paltry dollars that is probably its honest worth." Aunt Vera said that she was sure some nice person would have found it and that I would have no trouble getting it back, and that was the way we left it. Aunt Vera means well every time.

After supper I decided to stay away from the Haywoods for a while, even though they are the only other people living right on The Hill. Usually I would drop over after supper for a few words with Jack or with Ellen if she happened to be around, or stay and see something on their TV with the whole family, if there was something worth watching. But it was not a thing I always did, so I decided I would stay home this time instead and see what interesting business might be going on around the rest of the world, according to my Star Roamer set and with what the sunspots would allow.

Sometimes about all I can get on the short-wave band of my set is static of the worst sort, and I have learned that this is largely radio-wave interference caused by the sunspots acting up. I got this information straight from the horse's mouth, so to speak, that being our science teacher at school, about whom I am only being polite when I refer to him as a horse's mouth. He is all facts and no imagination and pretty bitter about it. He's the sort who likes to keep reminding people that the world will not last forever after all. That's how I found out about sunspots, when there are flareups or explosions of a sort around the edges of the sun. He pointed out that these may someday get pretty serious and even now they can louse up radio signals all around the world. He gave us a whole lecture on it proving that either these sunspots or other astral variations would someday wipe us clean out of the universe. This seemed to please him, oddly enough. It bugged me enough so that when the class was over and he was gone, I went up and wrote big across the blackboard, *If the sunspots don't get you,*

49

the astral variations will, so prepare to die! and signed it *Sad Sam Brooks,* which was his name, Mr. Samuel Brooks, Jr. I got in some minor trouble over this, but I thought it was worth it.

What brought this to mind was the way all I could get on my set around the world this time was squawks and squeaks and static, except for a few shrimp boats out in the Gulf having a boring discussion on band three about whether there might be a thunderstorm coming up or not. I finally gave up and went to band two, which is regular AM radio, and got some decent music, which I turned down low and listened to without the phones, stretched out on the bed wishing there was more of a breeze and trying to put all the events of the day altogether out of my mind. Tired as I was from that swim, it was not an easy day to forget; it kept breaking in on my thoughts every time I moved a muscle and felt it hurt and remembered why. So I stretched out as still as I could and tried to pay attention to the music and waited for it to get late enough so that I could go to bed without having it seem odd.

Finally a little breeze sprang up and I was just getting comfortable from the heat of the day when I heard the squeak of the back gate swinging open. Well, I thought, I suppose Jack has just remembered another country item for my education, and I waited, but instead of the sound of his feet pounding up the back steps to the porch, there was no sound at all. There is a low wooden wall that runs around the porch that I cannot see over without sitting up, but the rest of the porch is only screened, so I can generally hear Jack thumping along from the time he slams open the gate and heads for the porch, and the quiet this time surprised me. Then right outside the porch next to my bed, so close it half startled me, Ellen's voice called out, as soft and easy as though we had been having a conversation right along. "That is certainly nice music, Rodney. Is it from far off?"

I got up and went to the screen and there was Ellen, all right, standing there in the dark as natural as could be, as though she always came over like this for a conversation now and then, though she had never done it before in my life. "Only from Mobile," I said, answering her question. "The sunspots tonight are something awful." I knew right away that that must sound pretty crazy to her unless she knew about sunspots and static, and I guess it did, because she laughed.

"Someday I'll figure that out, I am sure," she said, "but here around The Hill anyhow there is a nice first quarter of a moon that will be setting pretty soon, if you would like to see it. I just noticed it myself and thought I'd stop by. It's right at the edge of the pines on the hill, and that always makes such a pretty sight, I think. Unless you are too tired, of course."

"I'm fine," I said. "I will find my shoes and be right out."

"Come barefoot if you want," Ellen said. "I am."

So I stopped looking around for my shoes and went out and found Ellen waiting in the dark, and for some reason I was a little flustered and all I could think of to say was that I was glad she had thought to drop by and something foolish about how nice the wet grass felt on my bare feet, hot as it still was.

"What I like best," Ellen said, "is the feel of the powdery dust in the road. It's dirty of course, but it feels clean even so." We walked out into the road between our houses, which is really just a kind of lane and mostly grass, and then out to the road that runs along in front, and there I saw what she meant about the dust, and how pretty the moon was, as perfect a crescent as if it had been drawn there, hanging low in the sky right at the tops of the pines on the top of the hill and lighting them up so that you could have counted the tops of each one if you had wanted to, while elsewhere the woods were more like shadows than like trees.

"Well," I said, "this sure beats sunspots any time," and then we walked down along the road a ways while I told her about sunspots and astral variations and static around the world, just to make conversation, although it seemed like a strange thing to be mentioning walking barefoot through the dust, with off to one side the moon already starting down behind the pines, almost close enough to touch, it seemed.

I was still a little surprised about Ellen stopping by for me, so I kept talking away for a while to cover it up, but finally we came to the bridge over the brook that runs into my uncle's pasture, where we stopped and leaned on the wooden railing and Ellen said, "Listen to the night things," and I got quiet. There were all sorts of insects and other small creatures unknown to me, possibly some of them frogs of one sort or another, making all sorts of noises, both soft and loud, and all of it making one general kind of racket that was nice enough and kind of impressive if you stopped and listened to it with some care. Then Ellen said, "Most all of that sound is really a kind of singing. But I expect you know that."

"I had never thought about it before," I said. "From things you can't even see, anyhow, it's quite a racket." I had suspected from the first that Ellen might have actually come by because I'd acted like such a kid about losing the skiff and was going out of her way to be nice to me, the way it used to be before, the first summer I was at The Hill and had done some similar stupid thing and went around moping about it. So I said nothing about the lost skiff and kept hoping that she wouldn't, either.

If she wanted to listen to the night things, that was fine with me. I noticed her watching me for a minute in the dark, and then she looked back out at the little creek and the swamp, which was all mostly one big shadow now, with the moon almost gone and the only light being starlight. "In the spring," Ellen said, "it can sometimes give me goose flesh. I guess that's silly, but it's so. It's just one big song. You can hardly hear yourself think. Even Ma and Pa come down just to listen sometimes."

"They do?" I said.

I turned and caught Ellen glancing at me again in the dark. Somehow, I could see her better now, as though I was getting used to just starlight. Also, it seemed that she had moved closer to me. In a way she was just a shape in the dark beside me, but in another way, in only starlight, all the realness, the particular beauty of hers, had never seemed more clear to me. Then I noticed that it seemed as though the night sounds were getting clearer, too, although maybe I was only getting more used to listening. "Yes, Rodney, they do," Ellen said. "To listen to the joy, Ma says."

The way Ellen said it, it surprised me, as though I really hadn't been listening, not to either her or the night things, and for a time I was quiet, not so much thinking as just listening, to the singing and to what Ellen had said, which was still sort of ringing in my ears. And for some reason the lost skiff seemed a small matter, and I thought, well, what if I have made a fool of myself today, here I am with Ellen, even so. And then the singing seemed to lift up again, louder and more mixed up than it had ever been yet, and then with a kind of sudden surprise it came to me clear and beyond any doubt that what I was listening to and hadn't known it, what the song was the night things were singing, was one big unmistakable love song. And I knew that Ellen had known it all along. And without meaning to I turned and found Ellen waiting in the dark, and with some confusion at first but then in the most natural way in the world, quick and hard and yet easy, I did what I had never dreamed that I could ever do. I held her close and I kissed her.

I guess it must have surprised her, but even so it had not been just a one-way thing at the end, sudden and short as it had been. Then she stepped back and gave her head a little shake and said, "Why, Rodney," as though she was certainly surprised, all right, and then she said, "How nice you did that," and that was all she said. I had not made a fool of myself, it seemed; and for a while after that we didn't say much of anything, just listened some more to the singing. Then we noticed it was getting late, and we went home, talking about this and that as though nothing at all had happened, with still no mention of the skiff, walking along in the dark, barefoot in the dust, with only the stars for light and no trouble at all.

6

When I woke up early the next morning all my tiredness was gone and I felt altogether confused, but apart from that, fine. I even tried singing while I was brushing my teeth at the sink on the porch, and my Aunt Vera came out of the kitchen and stood looking up at me with such a worried look I had to laugh. No telling what was going on in her mind. She must have known by then that her own husband was surely a strange one and I was a Blankhard, too; she could have stood there wondering if the Blankhard blood had produced another nut. So I went over and gave her a hug, which I do occasionally anyhow, feeling that life has been none too kind to her, and not wanting her to think that all the Blankhards in the world are altogether lacking in feelings or imagination. And anyhow, I like her. "Nothing like a good night's sleep," I said, and that seemed to satisfy her.

To tell the truth I had waked up with Ellen and the matter of the lost skiff all mixed up in my mind in a pretty crazy way. Since the moment I had lost the skiff it had been nothing but a hang-up to me, every time I thought of it, but now I had waked up positively excited about it and thinking that I could hardly wait to get looking for it, like this would surely be nothing but fun and certain to succeed. And all the time I was thinking this I was thinking about Ellen as well, although not nearly so clearly, just thinking about her and feeling more amazed, I guess, than anything else, and knowing that the matter of Ellen was in no way as simple as the matter of the lost skiff, although what the one thing had to do with the other was something that made no sense at all as far as I could see.

After breakfast my confusion remained but I decided to

stop worrying about it. I was sure of one thing. The things that had happened had happened. All of them. And all in one day. No wonder I'm confused, I thought. But this is a new day, and what will happen next I'll have to wait and see. None of the things that had already happened had been planned that way, so I saw no point in trying to see too far ahead. It seemed to me, in my experience at least, that life when it is either good or bad can sometimes be very much a matter of surprises.

So I decided that I had a lost skiff to find and I would do my best to find it, and that would be the most that I could do about that. If it had sunk and gone to the bottom somewhere, I could look forever and never find it, so it wasn't altogether up to me. And with Ellen, as much as I dared to look ahead, this seemed a good way to look at it, too; that it wasn't altogether up to me. For good or bad, though, I had learned enough, I believed, to count at least on some more surprises; seemed like they just came natural to me.

As a good example, I had just finished making my bed and straightening up around the porch some when Jack came walking up the steps hardly making a sound and opened the door without slamming it and came over and sat down in the chair in front of my Star Roamer set. Which was a little thing, all right, but enough of a surprise to me that for a while I didn't know what to say. He just sat there staring at the set, which wasn't even turned on, almost like he was mad at it and had come over with his mind made up to finally solve its mysteries for once and for all. He hadn't so much as said hello to me. And then finally, still staring at the set, he said, "I wish someone would explain a thing or two to me. I am not an idiot."

"Jack," I said, "I have explained that radio to you the best I can, and you have read the little book that came with it as well. I may have found you somewhat slow about it, but I have never said you were an idiot or even thought it."

Jack reached over then and turned on the main switch. "Thank you very much," he said. "But I am not talking about this little old toy radio of yours."

"Oh," I said. "I see you have just turned it on. Good for you."

"A kid could work this thing," Jack said, "with practice. If I had knowed it was worrying you so, I would have mastered it long ago. What I would like explained is something probably far beyond your brains to handle. And if we are going to get sarcastic about who is stupid, remember that I can break you in two like a dry stick, which if you was bald is just what you would look like."

Jack doesn't like being puzzled. Although a puzzle is not an easy thing to bring to his attention, once he gets tangled in it and can't figure it out, it comes to seem a kind of insult to him. I had seen it happen before. Then he finds it necessary to remind the world how strong he is, which is a fact; but with me it has never been more than threats.

"I am trembling and faint with fear," I said. "Watch and I will fall to the floor unconscious. What is it that has flown up your tail this morning?"

"Your Uncle Charles, for one thing," he said. "He has had Pa by the ear for the last hour and it don't make sense. Pa don't. Or Ellen, either. Your Aunt Vera just sits there. Nodding yes. Don't she ever nod no once in a while?" Then he reached down and pulled the phone jack out and gave me a sly grin and turned the dial and got it on band two and got a Mobile station loud and clear.

"That's Mobile," I said.

"Think of the mystery of it," Jack said, being sarcastic, then he turned down the volume. "Last night I argued with Pa all evening trying to get him to see that we ought to get back up on the creek the sooner the better if we was to ever find the skiff you lost of his. And Ellen makes it her business somehow and says why there is no hurry, it will probably be returned anyhow, and poor Rodney needs some rest and all sorts of nonsense more or less in agreement with Pa's feeling on the matter. I was finally reminded to shut up about it and told that we couldn't go up there because of the need of work around the place until a week from today, which is way next

Monday, and that was final. But now all of that is changed, and it don't make sense. Generally speaking, your Uncle Charles, if you want the truth, could not convince my pa of the time of day, or Ellen, either. But you can go over there now and there he sits saying all the things to Pa I said last night, with Ellen sitting there nodding yes to everything he says twice as hard as your Aunt Vera, and even adding some new arguments of her own to Mr. Blankhard's. For no reason at all, she has changed her mind completely. And while Pa so far is just sitting there being polite to your uncle I can see he is giving ground and will probably start in nodding yes pretty soon himself.

"So I guess we better start making up a list of what to take. At your uncle's expense, he says, so we can make it a big list if you want. But what has got Ellen to change her mind like that is something she won't even give me a hint about. Like she does not even trust her own brother. So I would like a thing or two explained, just for my own satisfaction. I do not like being taken for a fool. Not by my own family and friends anyhow. The only suspicion that has come to my mind is that maybe you have gone to Ellen begging her to do this for your sake, though I am sure you would not admit it if it was true and so I am probably wasting my time. But I can't think of nothing else that makes sense at all. Did you?"

"No," I said.

"I knowed you would say no," Jack said.

"I have not mentioned the skiff to Ellen since I have been home," I said. "And that's the truth."

Jack looked at me hard and was quiet for a time, and then he said, "I'm not saying you're a liar, but you are no more telling me the truth than Ellen was. Or why have you went so white?"

There was nothing I could do about turning white and I knew it; the only thing I could do was lie. I thought fast and then I said, "I guess I was not listening too good. I am still tired from yesterday. That was a long swim. It's hard to get it out of my mind. I couldn't help remembering one thing just now while you were talking. I haven't told you about it, but I was swimming on my back and resting when these floating pine needles slapped up against my ear. To be honest, it scared the hell out of me. I guess that's why I turned white. It's the only thing I can think of."

"I sure would liked to have seen that," Jack said. "Anyhow it is really nothing. I guess if people want to lie to me now and then it's no business of mine. And maybe you have told the truth. The best thing is probably to forget it and hope that Ellen does not decide to change her mind again for some mysterious reason. Have you got started on a list yet? We will need lots of water for sure, as the water down on Big Star Creek is not fit to drink, and being out on water in the sun can give you a thirst that would surprise you."

"Nothing surprises me," I said, and Jack looked at me odd, and I said, "But you are right. We must not forget water." I hunted around on my desk and found a pencil and pad and wrote down *water,* and then I sat on the bed and Jack sat in the chair and we went to work making up a list.

Jack must have spent the whole night lying awake thinking up a plan. "I had figured being gone three days," Jack said, "if we was going to row, and I guess we are as Pa says the motor is not to be trusted any more. So we will leave it at three days but plan for five, as long as your uncle feels it is his duty, as he told Pa, to make sure us boys is well equipped as far as our safety and domestic needs is concerned for the time it might take us in our search. Pa really batted his eyes some at that one. Sounded like it had been read out of a book. So now we can plan to stop and fish some and take our time and have some fun as well as work and depending on the weather figure an easy three days down, keeping to the west bank all the way, after the Little Star gets to be the Big Star, and two days coming back along the east bank, with maybe staying a day at the point down at the basin if we find the skiff early or make better time than I believe we will. How does that sound to you?"

I had heard him all right, but without giving it any

thought. "That sounds fine," I said. "I had figured on four or five days myself."

"We will figure five for the list we are making anyhow," Jack said, and then he started naming off the numbers of different kinds of canned foods he thought we should take, and other items, and I was kept busy just writing it all down. I wish I had been paying more attention, because I noticed some of the items I was writing down, like Polish sausage and three cans of collards and a small bucket of lard, didn't sound like items I would be apt to have a taste for. But since Jack had already worked it out I just went on writing down whatever he said and trying not to let him guess how much more than he was I was puzzled by the way Ellen had changed her mind and seemed in such a big hurry now to get us up on the creek and out of sight. If Jack had only known, it made a hell of a lot less sense, or maybe more sense, to me than he could have ever guessed at. Why it should have bothered Jack so, I didn't know; but I knew why it bothered me, and I knew I would somehow have to get the answer to it if it was to be the last thing I ever did.

To tell the truth, knowing only what I knew and no more, there was a plain hard hurt to it that I could not deny. And it made the whole business of looking for a lost skiff seem more or less like kid stuff, so I left it up to Jack and just kept nodding or saying "good" or "right" and agreeing with anything he said and writing it all down. It must have taken us a good hour, what with Jack changing his mind every so often and then having me stop and read the list back to him, but finally Jack said he couldn't think of a thing he had forgot and we called it done. It was quite a list.

Then Jack got to wondering out loud some more about how come his sister should have changed her mind so overnight, when usually once she had taken a side against him she would stick to it no matter how wrong she was or no matter what. "Why let it bug you?" I said. "Anyhow, I can't see that it's any business of mine." I was anxious to get him off the subject altogether.

"If you have not been lying all along," Jack said, "then I

suppose you are right at that. But you have not knowed Ellen the way I have, either, or you would understand how much she took me by surprise."

Well, I thought, you might also be surprised to know how well I have come to know your sister, although less than an hour or so ago I would have been a little more certain of this myself; but I could tell you a thing or two about surprises, such as you hardly get used to one when you get clobbered with several more. But all I said was, "For whatever the reason, the sooner we get started looking for that skiff I lost the better I'll like it," which was pretty much a lie, as I could tell by the phony sound of my voice, but which Jack seemed not to notice.

And then Uncle Charles and Aunt Vera came in through the front door and Uncle Charles said to her, "I will go and tell the boys to start making preparations," and he came back out to the porch and made a kind of announcement, saying that he and Mr. Haywood had consulted together on the matter of the lost skiff and were of a single mind that the sooner a thorough search for it was commenced the better it would be, and that he, my Uncle Charles, would see to it that we were properly supplied, being that I was the responsible party through whose negligence the skiff had been lost. "If you boys will prepare a list of necessary items needed to be purchased, your aunt and I will take care of it when we go into town with Mr. Haywood this afternoon. I have in mind only items necessary to your health and safety of course."

"We have got a list already worked up," I said, "adequate to our purposes, I believe." Sometimes when I talk to my Uncle Charles I find I have ended up sounding just like him. It bugs me. I had separated the list of things we already had on hand, like a tarp and fishing equipment and things of that nature, and made a separate list of things to be bought, mostly food. So I handed him this list and Jack and I stood back a bit to watch the results. For a while he just stood there looking at it and nodding his head up and down, although I don't think he was really reading it yet, but just taking in the fact of its length. Then he gave us both a quick kind of questioning look, with a small sort of imitation smile on his face, as though there was a chance that we might be joking. And then he turned and walked into the other room, where he was quiet for a time, finally reading it item for item, I guess. Then he came back. "May I ask how long you boys intend to be gone?" he said.

"Five days at the most, but more likely three," Jack said.

"Well," my uncle said, "I would say that this list of food-stuffs is adequate to some unforeseen emergency needs of the entire population of both families here on The Hill for a week at the minimum."

"We have naturally figured it so as to be on the safe side," Jack said. "You will notice most of it is canned stuff that can be brought back if not needed, which you could then eat up yourself. Or else save it in case of an emergency, like you mentioned. We plan to waste none of it however, I can promise you that."

"We have given some thought to all possibilities, including bad weather," I said. "You can see that for yourself."

"Living out in the open," Jack says, "it picks up the appetite every time."

"Yes," Uncle Charles said, and for a while that was all he said, as he had gone back to studying the list again, and then, reading from it, he said, "Suntan lotion?"

"For Rodney," Jack said. "He burns. And there is not much shade out on the water."

"That is true," my uncle said, "in both instances."

"We have thought of everything," Jack said. "The lard is for frying fish."

"I had wondered about the need for a bucket of lard," my uncle said. "But I suppose it can be brought back for later use along with the other items, if unused."

"If it don't turn rancid," Jack said, "but that's a gamble we will have to take."

Then Uncle Charles went through the list asking about this thing and that, until I felt sorry for him, and Jack and me both said a few cans less of one thing and another would do, until he seemed at last to be satisfied that he had done the best

61

he could with it. "Now of course," he said, finally, "there is one item here that I have not mentioned because surely it was included as a joke. I am referring to the item of six cheap cigars. Naturally I would supply you two young boys with no such a thing."

"Ha," Jack said, "you have misunderstood. Them six cigars are strictly for the matter of our protection and health."

"You don't say," said my uncle, "as an antidote to snake bite I presume, to be chewed up and swallowed?"

"I have heard of it being used like that for poison-oak rash," Jack said, "only regular chewing tobacco rather than cigars is used and it is not swallowed but chewed up and spit out and rubbed on the rash. Myself, I would as soon keep the rash as to trust in such a filthy cure."

"We are certainly in agreement there, Jack," Uncle Charles said, "but I am still at a loss as to how six cheap cigars may be employed to the end of your protection and health."

"It depends on the insects," Jack said, "the biting ones. If they are bad, we could both of us come back as prickly with bites as a couple of cucumbers and wore out from the bother. But the one thing insects cannot stand is the smoke from cheap cigars. Only man can stand it, I guess. I believe if used right it would hold back a mad dog. But it is only the insects that we was preparing for."

"I see," my uncle said. "I suppose you light the cigars and wave them around until the insects are all repelled? Or is it necessary actually to smoke the cigars?"

"What you do," said Jack, "you light the cigar and suck in the smoke and blow it out, as much of it as you can stand yourself. It is painful, but is the only satisfactory way that I know of to do it."

"And you do not consider that smoking a cigar?"

"Well," Jack said, "there is no pleasure in it, for sure."

My uncle nodded, and then he said, "I trust your innocence, young man, if not your logic, but I fear you will have to battle the insect world through other means, at least at my expense. I will substitute instead of six cheap cigars a large bottle of insect repellent."

"I will use it if we have to," Jack said, "but if the yellow flies is still around I know for a fact they will come to us in swarms, drawn by the smell of it, like gnats to fresh blood. Cigars is best."

For a moment I thought my uncle had almost smiled, and then he said, "Cigars, Jack, I am sorry to say, *is* out." Then he discussed our other preparations with us until he seemed satisfied that we had seen to our safety as well as to our hunger, and then he left us to go on with our preparations by ourselves.

It turned out to be a job that took us most of the rest of the day, mostly because when Jack thought he knew right where something was, he didn't, like the old tarp for the back of the pickup, which Jack believed was stored in the back of the pump house but which we finally found after about an hour of looking under a bench in the tool shed. Still it kept us busy and used up time and kept me from thinking too much about other things. I managed not to go into the Haywoods' house at all, and not once until evening did I happen to see Ellen.

Jack and I were out at the side of his house putting the last of our stuff in the back of the pickup, along with all the stuff they had brought back from town for our trip, when Ellen came down from the porch and came around and stood there watching us for a time. Then Jack remembered he had forgot his tackle box, and he went into the house to get it while I started spreading the tarp out over the whole mess, just in case it should rain during the night. I was having trouble with it, which Ellen soon noticed. "Give me a hand to get up in back with you," she said, "and I will give you a hand with that tarp." So I gave her a hand and she swung up into the truck and we were face to face again for the first time since the night before.

The sun was coming in slanting down the road behind us, lightening it all up with evening light, but we were out of it, and in the shade of the house and the shadowy light of evening around us her face stood out sort of pale and clear, and it seemed that her eyes were darker than I had ever noticed before. I guess I just stood there still holding her hand and

63

staring down at her for a time, and then she gave my hand an unmistakable squeeze, although soft as could be. "I will miss you, Rodney, while you're away," she said.

"Well," I said, "I would like to stay awhile longer, but the sooner we get looking for that skiff the sooner we will be apt to find it." And then with my confusion even worse than before, we went to work getting the tarp spread out and fastened down all around and soon had it done. Then we sat on opposite sides of the edges of the truck talking and waiting for Jack to come back with his tackle box. Ellen noticed that we were leaving well supplied at least, and with a good plan, it seemed, to have been worked up on such quick notice. And I almost came out and asked her about that, but I thought better of it, because if for some reason she had wanted me gone for the next few days there seemed no point in making her either deny it or come right out and say so. So I said nothing except that I sure did hope we would find her father's skiff.

"Whether you find it or not," Ellen said, "it should be an adventure. That is a long river, and except for Jack you will be alone."

We were quiet for a while and then I noticed the last of the sunlight was gone from the road, and finally I said, "I don't mean anything against Jack at all, but in a way, I wish I was going just by myself. Just to prove I could do it."

"I am sure you could do it," Ellen said, "no matter what."

And I didn't know quite what to say to that, particularly the nice way Ellen had said it, not just as though it was something friendly to say, but as if she meant it. I couldn't help wondering why she had first come out and then stayed, just to be with me, it seemed, if for some reason or other she had changed her mind about me after the night before, the way she had changed her mind about getting us off looking for the skiff in such a hurry. So finally I said, "Well, even with Jack along I expect it will be something of an adventure. There are always surprises in store for me, it seems." I looked out at the road as though I was speaking more or less generally and then I looked across at Ellen and she had stopped smiling and looked as though she was waiting for me to say something more or to explain myself. "When I get back," I said, "maybe we can talk about it some," and then not altogether sure just what I was referring to myself, I said, "And if your kid brother cannot find that tackle box of his, maybe they will let me go on by myself at that."

"When you get back," Ellen said, "I'll be glad to find out about everything that happened. I guess you know, but a trip like that will hardly ever turn out just the way you planned. And I've told Jack and I will ask it of you, too; please, Rodney, if a lightning storm comes up, the way they do so often in the late afternoons this time of year, will you please not stay out in the middle of the river, a natural target. Try and find some shelter somewhere along the bank and be patient and wait for it to pass. I am scared to death of lightning."

"Don't worry, Ellen," I said. "I know nothing about nature, but when it comes to lightning I get the message plain enough. I am a great respecter of lightning myself."

"Ma will be pleased to hear that," Ellen said. "Sometimes I think that Jack has not got the sense to be afraid of anything. Even lightning."

Then Jack came out with his tackle box in one hand and something long wrapped up in a blanket in the other hand; and the way he quick stuck them in under the tarp made me suspicious right away, and Ellen, too. "What is it wrapped up in the blanket that you are being so sneaky about, Jack Haywood?" Ellen said.

Jack just looked at her for a while, and then he said, "Can't you ever not notice something?"

"What took you so long?" I said.

Jack gave a sigh and flung up his hands. "What took me so long," he said, "was waiting for Ellen to find something useful to do, so I could sneak my rifle out and put it in the truck." He turned to Ellen. "For our safety and protection," he said. "Now go ahead and scream for Ma."

So Ellen turned toward the house and let out a yell for her mother that startled me. "Ma," she yelled, "you better come talk to Jack."

The next thing I knew both Mr. and Mrs. Haywood were at the truck, and finally even my Uncle Charles. Mr. Haywood was half for letting Jack take the rifle, arguing that it was only a twenty-two and might be useful against snakes, while Mrs. Haywood argued back that Jack would probably see nothing more harmful to shoot at than innocent songbirds, and shooting at them he could just as easy shoot me or himself, and that if that rifle went along with two mere boys all alone for five long days in the woods, then she went, too. Uncle Charles was not on either side, exactly, although he clearly had a suspicion that a gun could more likely mean some new trouble and expense rather than the lack of it. I left before they had worked it out, without saying good-by to Ellen or even seeing her again, as she had gone on into the house as soon as she had hollered for her mother.

We left for The Landing before daybreak the next morning, Mr. Haywood and Jack and me. Without Mrs. Haywood and without Jack's twenty-two rifle. I was just as satisfied. All I was hunting was Mr. Haywood's skiff. I could see it was a setback to Jack though. "What if a water moccasin gets into the boat with us?" Jack said to no one in particular sometime after we had left. "Do we just jump overboard and swim for shore?"

Mr. Haywood looked at Jack and then back at the road and seemed to be thinking about it awhile and then he said, also to no one in particular, "If a moccasin gets in a boat, and you have a rifle, the normal thing to do is to grab up your rifle and shoot at the snake until you have shot it dead, allowing for a number of misses and minor wounds. And when the snake is finally dead and your boat is sinking from being shot full of holes, *then* you swim for shore. That is the advantage of a gun."

It looked like Jack had finally brought Mr. Haywood altogether over onto Mrs. Haywood's side.

7

Sometime while we were still going straight up the highway, I went to sleep. It was still dark at the time and I had not slept very sound even for the little sleep I had been able to get. The truth is that I had lain awake trying to puzzle out the whole crazy business with Ellen, with my mind going around in circles and getting nowhere, and when I finally did get to sleep it was still just one big hang-up that wouldn't quit. So when I noticed Jack's head kind of nodding as we drove along, and with no one having any new observations to make since Mr. Haywood's observations about shooting snakes in boats, I finally got tired of staring out the window at nothing but a road and went to sleep.

When I woke up it was just turning light and the pickup was stopped in front of a restaurant that was all lit up, and right in front of us was a big sign that said TRUCK STOP and under that EAT. I looked around and we were wedged in among more big trucks than I could count, mostly those enormous cross-country diesel jobs. It was like I had waked up and discovered I was a midget. Jack was sleeping away beside me. Mr. Haywood was gone. I shook Jack and finally he came awake and looked around and said, "Holy cow, we have come too far."

Then Mr. Haywood came up out of someplace and said, "All right, it's time for breakfast, boys," and we followed him into the restaurant and he ordered us both two eggs and ham and grits and toast, and coffee and milk as well, the coffee being a kind of treat. "Eat up and enjoy it while you can," Mr. Haywood said. "I imagine you will remember this meal in the days to come." All he had for himself was a cup of coffee.

Then we were back in the pickup and ready to start back toward the turnoff to The Landing when Jack slapped his head and said, "Holy cow, I forgot to bring a toothbrush," which struck me as odd, because we had agreed not to bother with anything along this line except one comb for me. "Wait, and I will run back in there and buy some chewing gum instead," Jack said. So we waited and after a while he came back with several kinds of gum, and we started off for The Landing again, with Jack chewing on several sticks of gum and every now and then somehow making a smacking sound with it right in my ear in a way that was a nuisance.

It was full daylight but still early and fairly cool yet when we finally got to The Landing and started to unload all our stuff. It made quite a pile, spread out on the ground in the clearing. When it was done, Mr. Haywood stood looking down at it shaking his head. "Maybe you better put all this into the big boat," he said, "and tow it along behind the little one." I could see he was joking and so could Jack, but it was a big enough pile to both of us so as to hardly seem much of a joke at that.

We had planned to take the little red boat, but I could see that this would hardly be sensible, and Jack soon had it doped out this way, too. "It will slow us down and make it more work," he said, "but it looks like we will have to use the big boat after all. We might make it with the little one, but it would sure crowd us up; and if some fool should go shooting by us in a decent-size motorboat, we could easily end up swamped and possibly sunk."

Mr. Haywood agreed. Then he helped us get the big boat into the water and tied to the pier. "Well," he said, "I guess you're all set. In case of snake bite, stay calm and use the kit just like the directions say. If anything goes wrong, get somebody to get to a phone and call me; and then just wait until I get there. If you get back before Saturday, go up to Mr. Matthews' and he will send word in to me by young Matt, and I'll come for you. I will expect you back here by noon next Saturday, whether you have found my lost skiff or not. Not a day later, Jack, or there will be trouble for you for sure." He glanced over at the pile of stuff waiting to be loaded into the boat. "I would distribute that about some as you load it, if I were you," he said. Then he turned to me. "Whether you find the skiff or not, Rodney, will not matter too much to me, as I know you will have done the best you could to find it. And that's all a person can do." Then he climbed in the pickup and gave us a wave and was gone, and Jack and I were left alone in the clearing.

I wondered at the quiet around us and for a while we just stood there looking at each other and then I said, "I guess it's just in my mind, but does it seem to you to have got unusually quiet all of a sudden?"

Jack nodded. "I had noticed it myself. What it is, it is getting late in the morning and the birds have quit their racket. Listen and see if you hear one bird."

I could remember now that before there had been some birds singing away right along, and we stopped and listened and Jack was right. The clearing was quiet as a cave. "Well," Jack said, "that is a certain sign that the heat of the day is well on its way, so we had better move along and get that boat loaded and get headed down the creek. The farther down you go the better chance there is that you will come upon a breeze now and then."

So we tied the boat up close at both ends to hold it sideways to the pier and went to work loading our stuff aboard. Jack said he had done it before, so I lugged the stuff down to the pier and Jack loaded it, shoving most of our canned stuff up in under the back seat until the space was packed solid. To keep it out of the heat of the sun, he said. Then he put our fishing poles and tackle boxes up at the front, along with a frying pan and a couple of cooking pots, all of which he hung along on either side by some pieces of wire he had brought along for that purpose, to keep things out from underfoot. Then he put some other little odds and ends up under the front seat, and then stuffed our blankets in on top of that, and the tarp in on top of the whole works. "It could rain a thunderstorm now," Jack said, "and our blankets would not get wet a drop."

Loaded down the way it was, the boat was straining at the ropes, and I mentioned this to Jack. "We are in luck," he said, "the tide has just started out, so let us get the last of the stuff in and take advantage of it. Just throw it in the back and I will sort it out later." So I hurried and threw the last of the stuff on down to him, including an ax which landed behind him when his back was turned and gave him a scare, not just the bang it made but for what it might have done to the bottom of the boat. "That was stupid thing number one you have done," Jack said, "and we are still tied up at The Landing."

Then everything was in the boat and I got in the front and untied the rope that held it there while Jack worked at the one in back, having trouble with it for a time, and then he got it loose; and like an elevator easing up to a stop my end of the boat lifted up out of the water and hung there, and I looked down and saw that the back of the boat was lower down in the water than looked right to me. Then Jack said, "Stay where you are," and came crawling toward me over the seats, and by the time he reached me the boat was more or less level in the water again. We were starting to drift sideways on down away from The Landing, and Jack picked up an oar and worked the boat around so we were drifting backward, at least, and then he said, "Well, in the stupid department it seems like we have started off even, one for one. Like a fool I have went and overloaded us at the back. It was not the tide going out that had pulled the ropes so tight, but the weight. I should have had better sense."

So we drifted some more and I could tell by the way that Jack just sat there shaking his head at his own foolishness that there was no need for me to point it out to him, and finally I said, "Well, look at it this way, if my Uncle Charles had not been so stingy with our list, we could have gone right to the bottom." Then I laughed.

Jack looked at me and shook his head. "When you get through laughing," he said, "maybe we ought to distribute this stuff around from under the back seat. Like Pa said." So being lighter than Jack by a good forty pounds, I eased down to the back of the boat and started working stuff out from under the seat and handing it up to Jack, and in a short time we had it distributed all over the boat, and our problem was solved. Then I took the oars and turned the boat around right and we started moving along down the creek. "Well," Jack said, "you watch you don't run us into the bank, and I will watch for the lost skiff."

Jack was sitting on the back seat and seemed to be enjoying himself again, staring down the creek and turning his head from side to side and making a big deal of it, as though his eyes were sharp as an eagle's and it was all up to him. "We will both watch for the skiff," I said. "You watch for it ahead and I will watch for it behind, where you might have missed it."

"Just row," Jack said, "that is all you need to worry about." So I rowed and after a bit Jack said, "The gnats back here are a nuisance. Makes it hard to see." And then he reached in his pocket and pulled out a cigar that was all bent out of shape, and after a while he got it fairly straightened out and lit it up and blew out a big cloud of smoke. "These are not as cheap as I would have liked, because the cheaper they are the worse they stink, but they was the cheapest they had for sale back there at the truck stop." Then he reached in his pocket and pulled out several more. "I'm afraid I have mashed them up some, but they will have to do." Then he looked around and blew out another big cloud of smoke. "Well," he said, "I hope you are satisfied. We are on our way at last."

"In a stupid cloud of smoke," I said, but I was satisfied all right, and leaned into the oars in a way that felt good. For such a big old boat and loaded so heavy, it moved right along.

Now that we were actually on our way down the creek for the one purpose of seeing if I could find Mr. Haywood's lost skiff, it began to seem important to me again, the way it had at first. I soon noticed that Jack had stopped spying around at the landscape like some Indian scout in a movie, and was just looking around enjoying the scenery as though we were only out for the ride. By the time we reached the island, I believed he had forgot about the skiff altogether. This bugged me a

71

little, but on the other hand I figured that if it had been the way I really wanted it I would have been going down the creek without Jack along, and as far as I was concerned I decided that it was all right with me if he lay back on the tarp he had put behind him for a back rest and closed his eyes and went to sleep. So I just kept rowing easy and watching both shores and said nothing.

The day warmed up fast, but in the narrow part of the creek we still got a good bit of shade from the trees on either side, although around each bend as we came around it I could see the creek opening up and getting wider, the way I remembered it, with bigger and longer patches of sunlight waiting for us up ahead. It was a pretty sight in a way, with the water flat and smooth in the shade of the trees, and the trees reflected in the water, so that at times we would seem to be gliding along with trees both above us and below us, too, like we were on a kind of elevated parkway, except that it was a creek. And then up ahead when I glanced there would be patches and streaks of sunlight, with the same to be seen behind, and as long as the creek was narrow and we were moving along in a shady part it was a colorful and pretty sight, as well as being cool and quiet. In the sun, though, you felt the heat, and, surprisingly, things didn't seem to show up as clear, but seemed blurred, particularly at a distance. I guess it could have been mostly a matter of my eyes being somewhat weak and sensitive to light, like my father's.

I wondered if it was the cigar smoke that had quieted Jack down or if he was just naturally less loud around water, but I had better sense than to ask him about it. I was satisfied to go along being quiet for a change. Once we came to a sunny place where there was a turtle stretched out on a log, and I noticed him in time and just let the boat drift by without making a sound, and we had got so close when he did notice us that I could hear his claws scraping the log as he quick scrambled off the log and went plop into the water, a drop of not more than a foot or two, but a loud plop even so. Jack had noticed it, too. "I doubt if anything wild is more clumsy than a turtle," he said. "The only way they can seem to get down off a log is to fall off."

"For a turtle," I said, "that is probably as good a way as any."

"If you watch one walk," Jack said, "it is like watching a dog trying to scratch a flea in under his side where he can't reach. He just paws away and does his best; but it hardly makes sense. The same with the way a turtle swims, although I guess you have to say he can swim better than he walks, although either way he waddles."

"What have you got against turtles?" I said.

"They catch fish," Jack said.

This seemed to me to be no small feat for a creature that according to Jack could hardly swim, but I said nothing and we stayed quiet again for a while. But I decided that the next time I got a chance to watch a turtle swim I would take a closer look, and see if it was true that it waddled when it swam. It hardly seemed likely to me, but still, I have found it is sometimes surprising the things that Jack will have noticed and remembered right.

So we moved on down Little Star Creek, keeping to the shady side as it widened out, but coming more and more into long hot stretches of sun, and longer bends, where the sun would first be in your face and then at your side and then at your back, with the creek bending back again until the next thing you knew you were doing the same thing all over again. "We are being roasted all around," Jack said, complaining already, "like pigs on a spit."

The creek was still narrow enough so that we could stay to either side to catch what shade we could and still watch along both sides for the sight of the skiff caught in under some low-hanging limbs or bushes, or stuck aground in a marshy place, although only once had we come upon what could be called a stretch of marsh along one shore, and it had been a small one. Mostly, it was thick tangled woods on either side coming right up to the water's edge, with now and then a place where the ground lifted up a few feet above the level of the water, where

73

there would be bushes growing, too. Close to the banks the trees were generally pines of one sort or another, mostly cypress, according to Jack, although he was not sure of the names of the others; farther back where the ground was higher there were the regular pines such as grow everywhere around The Hill, loblolly pines, they are called, and others bigger and older-looking, which Jack said could be the true longleaf yellow pine, although most of it had been timbered out in this part of the country long ago. And now and then you would see, back from the creek, the big solid mass of green that only the flat wide leaves of a hardwood make, swamp maple and sweetgum and blackgum and hickory and others that Jack could not name at such a distance. "There are more oaks back in there than you can name," Jack said, "but the water oak is most common due to the fact of all this water. But there are live oaks, too, the ones like a big low cloud with the millions of small shiny leaves that don't look like an oak leaf at all. And red oak and white oak, which some call green oak, and post oak, with new kinds still coming along, according to Pa. I have give up on oaks a long time ago, except for the most common; but I will tell you this, if it has an acorn it is an oak, and if it don't have an acorn it is something else."

All I had done was ask Jack what kind of a tree it was that we had just gone under where it leaned out from the shore about one-third of the way across the creek. It looked like it must have been growing in several feet of water, and it was hard to believe that it could lean that far over and still have a good enough hold in the muddy creek bottom to keep it from falling the rest of the way down. I'm not so interested in trees that I would generally like to know all their different names and that sort of thing, but Jack had said that the tree I asked about was a cypress, and then he had gone on mentioning the different kinds of trees there were going by on either side as though I had asked him about the whole subject of trees.

But finally he quit. "To me," I said, "it still looks like one big mixed-up woods, with some of the trees pines of one sort or another and some of them not, but with the members of the pine family having the edge in numbers. But the one thing that seems positive to me is that it is not the kind of a woods that you go walking around in."

"You have figured something right for a change," Jack said. "Unless you could jump from limb to limb like a squirrel, of course. What those trees along both shores is mostly growing in is a matter of pure muck."

Then we were quiet again for a time and sooner than I had expected it we came to the clearing with the PRIVATE, KEEP OUT sign on it. "It is sure nice to come on a clearing and some solid ground now and then," Jack said. "Reminds you that the world is not just a place for fish and animals and bugs, but for people as well."

"To tell you the truth," I said, "I was relieved to find it here myself the day I lost the skiff."

"I bet you was," Jack said.

Then a little farther on we came to high ground again and then to the little overgrown clearing where I had landed and gone off following a game trail and come back to discover that Mr. Haywood's skiff was nowhere in sight. I stayed out in the creek but stopped rowing for a minute and said to Jack, "That's the place," and then we slowly drifted on by it.

"I figured it was," Jack said. "As you soon will see, there is not another place like it for quite a ways now. Just solid woods, growing up out of the water, it looks like, on both sides all the way, without a break or dry ground anywhere. You'll begin to notice a good bit of Spanish moss hanging down from the limbs, but otherwise there is little change, with nothing but trees, mostly cypress and some of the biggest you'll ever see, all jammed together with their roots in the muck, and with the creek not even widening out, it seems, but twisting and turning around through the woods like it was doing its best to get lost and end up nowhere."

"Sounds like it could get monotonous," I said.

"You will see," Jack said. "Along through here, according to Pa, you are probably seeing a sight still much the same as it was when first seen by man and even before."

"I will watch for it," I said. "As well as for the skiff."

Jack shook his head the way he will do sometimes when to

his mind I have shown my ignorance again. "You'll see," he said again. "Strange enough, it is a favorite with Ma. 'Here,' she says, 'we surely trespass.' And I believe her. To Ma, of course, it somehow has to do with God; but to me it is the loneliest, most awesome stretch of creek that I know of anywhere."

Then the clearing was out of sight and Jack offered to take the oars and I let him. It must have been about ten o'clock. "With me rowing," Jack said, "we should make the next clearing by noon."

8

Judging by the sun, we got to the clearing about when Jack had figured we would. In fact I was surprised at how right Jack had been about all of it. The stretch of creek we had finally covered was just as lonely and awesome and as wandering and lost-seeming as he had said it would be, but the more and more it went on the less you could say it was monotonous. It was something to wonder at. I would never have guessed that a little creek no bigger than this one could come to make you feel so small, the way a sky full of stars at night can do, or the Empire State Building, if you have not seen it up close before.

But then we finally came around the last sharp bend and could see the creek suddenly opening up on both sides and getting wider, and then the clearing coming in sight, a bright big piece of green cleared land, stretching away up an easy slope on solid ground; that was a sight to remember, too. And to land and pull the boat up safe and get out and walk around, it was like discovering land for the first time. It was a strange sensation, which I mentioned to Jack. "When I get this far," Jack said, "particularly if I have rowed and come alone, it always seems like I have come much further than I have, like I had been on that dark twisty stretch of creek forever. While actually it has not taken long, as you noticed, and as far as really getting somewhere, as far as this creek is concerned, you have hardly got good and started yet."

I looked back the way we had come. "I can see what you mean," I said. "All that twisting and turning is deceptive. On a straight line, so to speak, we have probably not come a mile."

"As the crow flies, probably even less," Jack said, back to

nonsense again, whether on purpose or by accident I wasn't sure. "But whatever time of day I get here, I am starved as one of your uncle's cats."

So we went down to the boat and got out one of the big jars of Polish sausages and a can of beans each and a box of crackers and some forks, and went back up to the back of the clearing where there was some shade. The tree we sat under was a live oak, a big one, and while all those acorns did not feel exactly like little cushions under me, the thousands of little leaves up over our heads were like a single solid roof, and the shade was a relief. I was uncertain about the sausage at first, but I tried one and it seemed pretty much the same as a Vienna sausage to me, except bigger, and while this is my idea of a food chiefly good for people without teeth, mushy as it is, I kept dipping in the jar for another one right along with Jack. "See," he said, "I knowed you would like them. We should have got more."

There were two more jars of them in the boat. "Well," I said, "they are all right, but I would not want them every meal." Between us, we finished the jar.

"I found out about these Polish sausages from Pa's Cousin Nat," Jack said. "Who you probably remember for his drinking. He would carry them around in his car, when he had one. Claimed they were the standard tavern food for drunks the world over and was all that kept many of them alive. So I turned down the whiskey he was offering me at the time and tried the sausage instead, although I might have tried the whiskey, too, except that this happened right on our own front porch, with Pa sitting there laughing and putting up with Nat, but keeping his eye on me as well. Well, before Nat had finished his whiskey and left that night I had finished the last of the sausages he had left in his jar, and have craved them ever since. Probably lucky for me I didn't try his whiskey, too."

"You are right," I said. "One thing can lead to another. All I hope is that I have not overdone it with these sausages already."

"Well," Jack said, "whenever Nat will come by with his

whiskey and his jar of sausages, Ma will generally say, 'I see Nat has brought along his baby food again,' meaning the sausage, I guess. So don't think of these sausages as food for drunks, but as baby food if you want. And what's good for a baby should give you no worry."

"I don't know how I could have made this trip without your tremendous help and wise advice, as well as your humorous stories to help keep my spirits up," I said, "but I would have liked to try. Even at the risk of loneliness and failure."

"Ha," Jack said, "I was wrong. Those sausages are clearly all caught sideways in your gut already. We better move on down the creek toward some civilization in case a doctor should be needed."

"I would just like to move on down the creek and get back to looking for your father's skiff," I said, "which is why we are here and not for a picnic, in case you have forgot." Then Jack took the two empty bean cans and heaved them off into the woods behind us. "Hey," I said, "you are littering up the woods."

"With two empty cans of beans?" Jack said. "I never knowed you was so neat. Anyhow they will have disappeared into rust long before they will be seen by another human eye. As you may have noticed, we have not so much as seen another soul so far today."

That was true, and I had noticed it all right. So I said nothing and watched Jack dump the last of the juices out of the sausage jar and then hang it from a small branch of the oak tree. "Well," I said, "I suppose you are waiting for me to ask why you have done that. So it can be seen from the creek? As a sign to the passers-by that other humans have been here? Or just to catch some acorns when they fall?"

"Just to liven things up a bit," Jack said, "for the jays. They is the most inquisitive bird in the world."

I had asked a silly question and got a silly answer, even if true, so we cleaned up the rest of our mess, which amounted to brushing the cracker crumbs off our clothes and washing our forks at the creek, and then we shoved off and started down the creek again, with me rowing, and Jack telling me a long story about how once his mother had put a sewing thimble on their gate post on her way over to see my Aunt Vera about something, while he had sat on the porch and pretty soon noticed a jay hopping around in the branches of the little dogwood next to the gate and looking down at the thimble and talking away to himself about it and then calling up other jays until finally the dogwood was bent down under the weight of blue jays, according to Jack, all hopping around and looking down at the thimble with first one eye and then the other and raising a racket among themselves, until finally one of them flew down and pecked at it and knocked it onto the ground and then another one flew down and picked it up and flew off toward the branch with it, with all the rest of the jays chasing after it, raising a racket until they were out of sight. Then his mother came back and looked around on the gate post for her thimble and down around on the ground, until finally Jack felt he had to tell her what had happened, knowing she wouldn't believe him. But to his surprise she had not the slightest doubt but that he had told her the truth. "What Ma said," Jack said, finishing it up, "was that I could not have made up such a clever lie and at the same time been so right about the nature of jays, which are as inquisitive as cats when it comes to something new, and not half so fearful of it."

I had only half listened, being busy rowing and keeping my eye out for the skiff, but I could see where Jack had not been altogether joking when he left that sausage jar hanging there from a limb. He had actually done it for the jays, even if he would never get to see if it had aroused their curiosity or not. It still seemed to me a pretty silly thing to do, but on the other hand, I figured that it had actually done no harm, while to Jack, he had got a kick out of it. It is not every day that you will find a kid who will take the trouble to kid some birds, and have the sense to know how to do it, and not even have to stay around to see if it works or not. So I saw no reason to knock it. Jack is sometimes a pest, but his way of seeing things is at least his own and sometimes not as dumb as it seems.

We had stayed in the shade at the clearing longer than we should have done, according to Jack, and would have to keep moving along steady if we wanted to reach a place to camp for the night before dark. The place he knew of, he said, was at a sharp bend where the creek had undercut the bank at a clearing years ago, and tumbled it into the water, and now there was a nice sandy beach there and bream beds, with some marsh grass across from it where the green trout liked to feed. "Bream for supper, if we get there in time," he said, "and with any kind of luck, green trout for breakfast." There would also be two small blackgum trees down by the creek, side by side, with a red-oak sapling already running from the lowest branch of one tree to the lowest branch of the other, unless whoever had put it there the year before had since come and taken it down. All we would have to do was throw our tarp over the sapling and we would be camping in style, with plenty of firewood right at our backs. Jack made it sound good, and I rowed right along.

The creek was slowly getting wider, but we could still see both shores clearly enough if I stayed out in the middle, which was not always the easiest thing to manage, as even if the creek was getting wider it still wasn't getting much straighter. And now there was no getting out of the sun for a minute. Without a breeze, the water was flat and like a mirror to the sky. And the quiet all around somehow didn't help much, either; we could have been wandering along in a desert for all the sense of loneliness and heat we had around us. The only sound was Jack, if he said something, or just the slow, steady creak and then the slipping sound of oarlocks turning back and forth as I kept rowing. I looked at the water as little as I could, and tried to watch the shores along either side, although the sun on a stretch of bright-green bushes bent out over the water could seem as shiny and as glittering with light as the water catching the sun when I lifted the oars at the end of a stroke. When I could, I tried to look back into the darkness of the woods, to rest my eyes from the glare, but the wider the creek became the more the woods on each side seemed like solid walls. Once, we passed a tall, dead tree sticking up all by itself in the middle of a marsh, with a bird Jack said was a king-fisher sitting at the top of it and never moving once in the long time it took us to go past, as though he was as dead for the time being as the tree itself, with even something in the way the feathers at the top of his head stuck out in back, as jagged as some of the dead limbs broken off the tree, making him look like he had sat there at the top of that tree and died along with it, struck by lightning, or just burned up, slower, by the sun. In the heat and stillness, even the fish seemed quiet, where during the morning you would every now and then hear the plop of a jumping fish or come around a bend and see the ripples still spreading out where one had jumped. But now, it seemed, we were all that was making a sound or a change in the scenery at all.

It was not as dark and the creek was not as twisty as it had been before we had reached the clearing at noon, but if we were moving toward some civilization on down the creek, we hadn't seen a sign of it by the middle of the afternoon. Not even somebody fishing or just out for a ride in their boat. I mentioned this to Jack. "No sensible person," he said, "would waste their time fishing at this time of day, or just go for a ride in this heat. Although I am surprised, to tell the truth, that we have not seen some fools by this time doing both. On a weekend, you would have seen at least a few Mobile people in their fancy motorboats by now. They cannot just haul them around behind their cars forever, so now and then you see them this far up the creek, usually blasting right along like they was out in the bay and had never heard of such a thing as snags. They will sometimes wave when they go by, but Pa just shakes his head."

Then Jack rowed for a while, and I sat in back and watched the creek slowly turning and twisting along ahead of us in the sun, with some shadows finally starting out now on the water here and there from along the shore. I kept watching for the skiff, but I believed along with Jack that by now it would have been taken in tow, and that we would find it, if we did, tied up at some landing farther down the creek. Still, I kept an eye out.

Finally I asked Jack when we would start running into some signs of civilization, and he said it would not be until after

Little Star Creek had got to be Big Star Creek. "Where does that happen?" I said.

Jack kept rowing, but he seemed to be thinking about it, and then he answered me. "As far as I know, there is no certain place. It's known as Big Star at the lower end and Little Star at the upper, and somewhere along the line I suppose it has to change. But where you start running into landings and then houses, all of that is on Big Star Creek. And we will not be there until tomorrow."

It seemed a strange way to me to name a creek, but I supposed that Jack was probably right about it. "Pretty soon," Jack said, "you will notice a good-sized creek coming into this one from the northeast, which is called Mud Turtle Creek by some and just Mud Creek or Turtle Creek by others, and there are some who say this is where Big Star takes off and Little Star ends. But if you look about you will notice there are no landings or houses and no change to speak of. And when we are on the Big Star part of the creek, you'll notice the change all right. For one thing, there will be some boats going up and down it, and some landings now and then." I could tell by the expression on Jack's face that I had brought up a puzzle he had not thought about before. Then he stopped rowing for a stroke, and looked about, and then he shook his head like he had settled it for himself, as much as he was going to, anyhow, and started back to rowing again. "You may have noticed by now," he said, "that this little old creek we are traveling down is not exactly U. S. Highway Number 98. It's just a creek. If you don't know where it is you are going on it, you wait and see. If you do know, you don't need no names or road signs."

"When I see some landings," I said, "I will figure we have left the Little Star behind."

"That won't be until tomorrow," Jack said. "And what has got me worried now is whether or not we will make the next clearing before we are apt to get some rain."

For the first time in hours, then, surprised, I looked up at the sky and around. The sun was still up there, bright and clear, although moving down in the sky, with all the sky clear as far as I could see, except for one big white cloud sticking up off in the distance like nothing more than a cloud of white-colored smoke. "Rain?" I said.

"For one thing," Jack said, "I don't like this stillness, and for another, I do not like at all that thunderhead you can see off to the west there."

"That one white cloud?" I said.

"That one," Jack said.

It looked a long way off to me, and the way I understood it, rain came from the dark clouds, while white ones were fine; but I decided I would not argue this with Jack. "You watch it," I said, "and I will row again for a while, and we will see."

Jack had been rowing at a good steady clip and I kept it the same, although I felt the pull of it up and down my back now each time I bent forward and then leaned back into the stroke. But I could see it hadn't been without effort for Jack, either, as he sat resting in the back, fanning himself with his Styrofoam helmet, and taking long drinks of water, one after another, and every now and then shaking his head to get rid of the sweat, like a dog shaking off water. Then he pulled off his jeans and jumped off the back of the boat and swam along beside it for a way. When he climbed back in, he just sat there on the back seat dripping, not even bothering to dry himself off.

The creek was slowly getting wider, and the shadows of the trees were starting to stretch out farther from the shore. The way the creek turned and twisted, sometimes the thunderhead Jack had noticed would be out of sight, and at other times, when the turn of the river was toward the west, without a near bank of trees blotting out the distance, then the thunderhead would be clear again, and looking bigger each time I saw it, still white as snow up near its top, but with a darkness farther down that looked darker and more spread out each time I saw it.

"I don't like the look of it," Jack said. "Sometimes a thunderhead like that will come up in the afternoon and only hang

84

there, doing nothing. Just something to look at. But another time it will build and move, and get blacker at the bottom while you watch it, and then you can be in for a storm. And there is a storm in this one all right. It's just a question of whether it is moving or not. If we had some wind I would know better about it. With an easy wind from the south, I would say we would get it sure."

"I suppose there is a reason you know of for that," I said.

"A good one," Jack said. "I have seen it happen."

"Oh," I said.

"You only have to remember," Jack said, "that the winds around a moving storm just naturally blow in a counterclockwise circle. The rest is a matter of figuring things out."

I kept rowing. After a while I noticed a creek behind us, off to my right, which I guessed was Mud Turtle Creek. Jack had said there would be no change, and I could see he was right. If I hadn't been watching for it, I might have missed it altogether. And then in a few more strokes of the oars it was out of sight behind a bend. "Well," Jack said, "I guess from here on we should move in close to the west bank and stay there, if we are serious about looking for the skiff. That's the bank on your left. While the sun may switch around and be sometimes on the right of you and sometimes on the left, or in front of you or behind you, for that matter, the left bank, facing back up the creek, is still the west bank, which is where we want to stay."

So, I thought, in Alabama, creeks change their names wherever they please, and a wind will blow one way while the storm will come another, and by sticking to the west bank you are apt to see the sun set in the east; and if I just keep rowing hard enough we may get to this wonderful clearing of Jack's before it gets dark or we get struck by lightning. I kept rowing.

Now and then we would pass close enough to the bank to move through some shade, and that helped. But then I noticed I was passing drifting leaves a good deal faster than I had been doing before, while at the same time it seemed that the shore passed by even slower, and the rowing seemed harder. "Jack," I said, "I believe the tide has changed and we are going against it now."

"I was waiting for you to notice it," Jack said. "You have been moving us right along, but I will take the oars for a while now, as we are in a race with time, against either a thunderstorm or night, whichever comes first."

"What about that clearing you talked about?" I said.

"It's where I said it was," Jack said, "which is still a good ways off."

From the back seat, I got a more regular view of the thunderhead now. It had spilled up higher and hung closer to us, with the sky around the sun darkening down to a kind of hazy purple color while the sky to this side of it, to the north, I guess, had gone altogether black. Then we moved out around a bend and onto a straight stretch of creek pointing straight toward the storm. And with the sun low in the sky but still bright and practically shining in my eyes, I saw a straight thin golden-colored streak of lightning dip down through the blackest part of the cloud. I waited and listened but there was no sound of thunder. "You won't believe this," I said, "but just now I saw a streak of lightning up ahead."

"I believe it all right," Jack said, "and I believe that before we are done with it you may see a good number more."

I started watching both shores as we kept moving along, wondering if there might at least be some dry ground where we could go ashore if we didn't make it in time to the clearing, but it was all a kind of swampy jungle again, and seemed to stay that way. And then in a matter of seconds all the brightness had left the sky and the shine was gone from the water and the green of the trees went dull, and the shadows stretching out from the trees along the shore beside me had changed to reflections. Off in the woods a bird sang and then stopped, like it had only meant to signal the change.

The dark cloud at the bottom of the thunderhead had finally moved up and blotted out the sun. The next streak of lightning I saw was bright and clear, and though it took a while, this time I heard the thunder. Jack heard it, too. "I wish," he said, "that we was one hour further down this stupid, lousy creek."

"What happens," I said, "if it rains before we get to that clearing?"

"We get our asses soaked," Jack said. "What the hell do you think?" It was clear that Jack did not like the looks of our situation at all. He only swears when a thing is no longer a joke to him.

"What about the lightning?" I said.

"There is nothing we can do about it," Jack said, "except stay in close to shore and take our chances. What I am worried about is the darkness and the storm both. There is no way to keep rowing on down a creek like this in the rain and darkness together. And I do not care for the idea of sitting in this boat tied up to some water oak along shore, with that heavy tarp hung over our heads, the rain pouring down and with the lightning to worry about, waiting for the rain to quit and the moon to give us some light. Or just waiting there for morning, like two rats in a barrel."

It didn't sound like a whole lot of fun to me, either. But from the way Jack rowed and from the look on his face, and the way the light kept fading away in the woods and up and down the creek, and the thunder followed the lightning louder and quicker each time, it began to look as if we might be in for a night just as bad as Jack had described it. It seemed to me, though, that with that big tarp we had brought, we should be able to do something better with it than just sit there holding it up with our heads.

I was still thinking about this when the first wind came, not hard, but making a kind of humming in the trees and then roughing up the water and turning it darker than it had already been. It was warm and gusty and you could feel the wetness in it, and then it picked up and got stronger and cooler. All the swampy smells of the river seemed to be blowing in it. Jack gave one big stroke with his oars that made the boat give a jerk, and then he just coasted, looking back up ahead of him at the sky, and at first one shore and then the other, and then he said, "There is no point in being foolish about it. We are not about to beat either the rain or the dark to that clearing, so we might as well take our time and find us some nice little tree to tie up to."

What we finally found was a small magnolia, more or less out and away from the taller trees back along the shore. We tied it close with the front line. "While we still got some time," Jack said, "we might as well eat." Now and then we would catch a glimpse of the lightning through the trees and the thunder was loud, but the sky was still clear straight up above our heads.

"Jack," I said, "I've been thinking about that tarp. One thing about it, it's big. With those rope holes all around it, it has given me an idea." The oars were still lying in the oar-locks where Jack had left them, with the handles back toward the front of the boat. I didn't know for sure if it would work or not, but I slid an oar forward and then shoved the pointed end of the handle back into a V-shaped place that had been cut out of a piece of the frame that came down the side of the boat and was joined to another piece going across the bottom of the boat to the other side. I wasn't sure whether this had been done to strengthen the joint or to let water in the boat run down out of its front end along each side, but I had noticed it, and the handle of the oar fit it perfectly. The way I'd done it, it left the blade of the oar sticking up in the air about three feet high along the side of the boat, and maybe two or three feet toward the rear past the middle seat. The thin edge was up, and that didn't look right to me, so I unwedged the oar and got the blade flat side up, and then I fixed the other one the same way.

Jack had been sitting on the back seat, watching me and not saying a word. "What do you think?" I said. "We can use some of that trotline cord of yours and tie the tarp to the ring in the bow and then just let it hang over each side of the boat and bring it on back and slide it up along the oars and tie it to each oar, and what is left over we can just stretch out over the back of the boat as far as it will go."

"Rodney," Jack said, "I take back everything I ever said

about how stupid you was. The only thing I can't figure out is why I never thought of it myself."

"Pure ignorance," I said, but it didn't seem to bother him. He even laughed. Then he grabbed up the tarp and we went to work, tying it up and stretching it out the way I had planned, and it was done without any trouble at all, except that Jack had to poke some holes in the tarp to tie it to the oars. The main thing was, it looked like it ought to work. There was only about two feet left of the tarp hanging down over the oars, and I was afraid the wind might get under it and give us trouble, but Jack fixed that by tying a couple of pieces of cord to the holes in the edge of the tarp and then opening the lid to the fish well on each side of the seat—the seat we sat on when we rowed was a fish well also—and tied the cord to the hinges of the seat. So what we had when we were finished was a kind of crazy V-shaped tent, about four and a half feet high at the front, figuring it from the bottom of the boat, with a tied-down flap at the front which lacked only about a foot of closing the tent in tight. It gave us room to squeeze in and out without untying the cords; and anyhow, I figured we would need the air. "Also," Jack said, "it will give us a view of the storm, which sounds like it ought to be a good one when it gets here, if it don't swing by us to the north after all."

It seemed to me that it was already right at our backs. I looked up and most of the light was gone from the sky, but I couldn't tell if it was the storm coming on or just the coming of darkness I was looking up at. While it was still light enough, we got the stuff out from under the tarp that wouldn't be hurt by the rain, mostly canned goods and pots and pans, and moved them to the other side of the middle seat. Then we fixed our blankets and tried them out. While it would be cramped, we could see it wouldn't really be bad at all. Then I took a quick swim to get the day's sweat off me, swimming out into the creek and seeing the lightning back off through the trees, and the white boat with its crazy tent, back in by the shore, and thinking, well, that is my home for the night, and then swimming back to it with really no great worry about the storm at all. Which surprised me.

When I'd got back in the boat and dried off, Jack had opened us each a can of tomatoes and of corned-beef hash, and with the last of the light we sat on the back seat and ate it all, cold, with the wind gusting cool and stronger all the time, and with the lightning close enough so that we could see it now and then lighting up the woods across the creek with a kind of soft, quick glow even though it had struck somewhere off behind us. I had never known cold canned food could taste so good; particularly the tomatoes.

Then it was dark, and I saw Jack looking up at the sky and I looked and there was nothing to see at all. "Well," Jack said, "there went our stars." And then I heard a new sound in the wind, like dry leaves blowing, it seemed, although it couldn't have been, and then the first few drops of rain slapped against my back and plunked around us in the water.

"And here comes our rain," I said. And right then the first close streak of lightning came, lighting up the creek and the woods around and holding for a time, with a kind of wavy light like the light of firelight, only brighter than the light of day. Then it was dark again, and right with the darkness the thunder came, with just a single, sharp clear bang.

Then we were in under the tarp, and the sound of the rain beating down on it was like a thunder all its own. "Now we will see if we get wet or not," Jack said, and then for a while we said nothing. It was enough to sit there, hearing the rain beating down and being stopped just inches from our heads, looking out through the opening in front at the night being ripped apart by lightning, and then darkness coming back, and then lightning again, with a quick, strange sight of the river still unchanged and the trees bending in the wind and shiny with rain, with sometimes the lightning being close, and then farther off, as though the storm was everywhere.

Then the lightning was less and its thunder seemed to be moving on back up the creek away from us, and the thunder of the rain on the tarp eased away to a kind of drone. "That was quick," Jack said, "but it was a good one. Was you scared?"

"Yes," I said.

"So was I," Jack said.

And then for a while we sat in the dark and listened to the storm moving off in the distance and to the droning, easy, safe-sounding noise of the rain, and after a while the strange thought came to me, that, like the creek and the woods all around, I had come through the storm pretty much unchanged, it seemed, but still somehow changed. I had been a part of it. Even being scared. Anyhow, I was almost sorry to hear it fading away up the creek, and for someone who would generally just as soon stay at home and explore the world with a short-wave radio, that seemed to me a surprising change.

What Jack was thinking I couldn't guess; probably nothing that odd. He just stayed quiet beside me, staring out under the tarp flap at the dark and the rain. Then he said, "The storm has gone, but no telling how long this rain will hang on. So maybe now we should have some light of our own. Just to see what we look like again."

I remembered where I had put the lantern up under the front seat, and I crawled up front and finally found it, and then Jack lit it, and set it up on the middle seat, and we sat looking around at the boat and the tarp and at each other, as though neither of us could think of a thing to say. And then finally Jack said, "So far, anyhow, we have not got wet a drop."

9

Once it had hit, I guess it did not take the thunderstorm more than a half an hour to move on past us; but though the rain eased up, it kept on. For a while we sat in the lantern light and talked about our plans for the morning. Whether it cleared up during the night or not, we decided to finish out the night right where we were. Then in the morning we could move on down to the clearing and with luck catch a green trout for breakfast, or anyhow have breakfast there, a cooked one, then go on down to the Big Star landings and maybe, with real luck, find the lost skiff.

It was still raining when we put out the lantern and decided to get some sleep. Several times I would be just about going to sleep and Jack would say something like, "Rodney, are your hands blistered yet?" or "Don't that rain sound nice?" or "Rodney? Have you noticed how the fish well keeps the water in the back of the boat from running in on us?" Always a question. Finally I said, "Jack, I wish you would be quiet."

"I will," he said, "but the sound of rain like that always gets me wondering about things. And I'm still wondering why Ellen was in such a big hurry to get us off up here to the creek." I had been thinking about that myself, off and on through most of the day, but I said nothing. "Have you ever floundered?" Jack said.

"No," I said, "but I know how it is done; with lights and gigs. Now we ought to get some sleep if we can."

"I'm sorry," Jack said. "I keep forgetting. But that is where Ellen is tonight, somewhere out floundering with Otis Duncan."

"Oh?" I said. What he said had caught me by surprise. But after that I just lay there awake, wondering, and waited.

Then Jack laughed to himself. "Do you know what a flounder looks like, Rodney?"

"Not exactly," I said.

"It has got these two eyes," Jack said, "off to one side in its lopsided head, and close together. And that is what Otis Duncan looks like, kind of lopsided, the way he keeps his hair so long and pushed over to one side, with those big close-up eyes of his. I cannot see what she sees in him."

"Who?" I said. It was stupid, but it seemed I had to say something.

"Ellen," he said. "Who else did you think I was talking about?" I didn't answer. I had known he meant Ellen, but it was though I hadn't quite believed it yet, or understood it right.

Jack was quiet for so long that I thought he had finally gone to sleep, and then he laughed to himself again. "Ha," he said, "maybe they will be getting some of this same storm themselves, and get their car stuck down at the end of some dirt road. While here we are, in no trouble at all."

I stayed quiet, pretending I was asleep, and then Jack said, "Rodney?"

"Goddamn it, Jack," I said. "Shut up."

I waited, and then Jack said, "Holy cow," low, like he was finally talking only to himself; and then pretty soon I heard him breathing slow and regular as though he had gone to sleep at last.

For a long time then I lay awake and listened to the rain, and thought. I thought about being fifteen, almost sixteen, and being stupid enough to be in some kind of love with a seventeen-year-old girl. Even one who, once, I had kissed. And who had kissed me back. She had; it was not something I had made up in my head. It had happened. And the truth, I thought, is that it had not meant a thing. Because naturally a seventeen-year-old girl is just fooling around if she is doing anything at all with a fifteen-year-old kid, even if he is taller than her. It is a damn sure bet, anyhow, that she is not going around eating her heart out for him. Not at the same time she is out floundering around at the end of some damn dirt road with some long-haired fish-faced country clod named Otis, of all the stupid names.

And at the same time I thought, you jerk you, did you really suppose that Ellen, a girl as pretty and wonderful as Ellen, would not seem interesting to some other boys, too, older boys, boys her own age, boys old enough to come out and ask her for a date? And did you really think there was some reason why she should not say yes if she wanted to, if the boy seemed nice enough, whatever he might actually have on his mind? She only paid you some attention now and then, I thought, and was friendly, and maybe laughed in a flirting kind of way sometimes, and let you kiss her once. She did not promise to marry you or love you or not have dates. And you have no damn reason to lie here half ready to cry like a stupid kid whose mother has just died or something. She was never your girl to start with. She never was.

For a while I tried not to think about it at all, just to listen to the rain and think about the skiff I was looking for and what the next day was going to be like, and if I had to remember something, to remember the lightning storm, the wildness of it, the realness, and the real difference I felt after it had passed, knowing something had happened and no doubt about it. And for a time I could make it work; and then the next thing I knew the sound of the rain would be the loneliest, saddest sound in the world and I would be thinking of Ellen again, and remembering Jack blabbing away in the dark not even knowing what he was telling me, never putting two and two together, not able to imagine why his sister was in such a hurry to get us off down a creek somewhere; so she could sneak off on a date and I wouldn't know it. No, I thought, to Jack I am just as much a stupid kid as he is, and of no more possible interest to Ellen. And even if I told him the truth he would probably just laugh and not believe it.

And then for a while I lay there thinking about this and getting mad at Jack about it, which made no sense at all, but I couldn't help it. For a while I even thought about waking him up. "Jack," I would say, "wake up and let me straighten you out on a few things and point out to you what a stupid jerk of a poor retarded kid you really are," and then I would tell him some things about what life is really all about and about sex and love and Ellen and me, and in the end I would say, "And now maybe you know why Ellen was in such a hurry to get me off The Hill; when it comes to me she is afraid of herself."

I could have made an awful fool of myself, but I knew better; it was clear I was acting like a pouty, poor little thumb-sucking kid just thinking such a silly daydream. And after a while I got disgusted with it and mad at myself instead of Jack and got honest again.

The simple truth is, I thought, Ellen does not have to sneak off from me to have a date. But she is not the kind of girl who would think it was funny to let herself be kissed one night by a kid she liked and who acted like he loved her, and then when he was still worried about her father's skiff, which he had lost, show him the next night that not only had he lost a skiff, he had also lost the girl he figured he just had found. And just leave him like that, kissed once, and all the rest lost. And thinking about this, I knew it was the truth. She had done it only to be kind. And I couldn't hate her for it. She was just trying not to hurt the feelings of a kid.

I kept thinking about it, and I knew I finally had it right. And I honored her for it, but it hurt like hell all the same.

And I figured that Jack hadn't meant any trouble, either. He hadn't even known what he was saying. I was just as glad he hadn't. But there was one thing left bothering me, that wouldn't quite let me get to sleep even after it seemed I had thought it all out the best I could and was satisfied to let it go. It was that one remark of Jack's, the last one, about Ellen and Otis Duncan being stuck in the mud down at the end of a dirt road somewhere. That just hung on in the back of my mind. And finally I thought, damn it, Jack, *everything* in this world is not somehow funny.

I guess it was the way he had laughed when the idea about it came to him that bothered me the most. I wished that once, anyhow, he had kept his mouth shut.

Then for a while longer I tried thinking about finding the skiff, and what lay ahead for me down the river, and I could only guess at it, but I did the best I could, trying to make better plans for what was to come, however little I knew about it. Then slowly the rain eased off and stopped, and I could hear it dripping off the leaves for a while longer onto the tarp and into the creek, until finally there was no sound at all, and I noticed a light at the opening in the tarp and I went and looked out.

High up in the sky there was a quarter-moon, clear as could be. It lit up the quiet woods with a kind of light that reminded me of White Plains and of winter and snow, and I wondered at how well known and yet far away all of that was. Yet it surprised me, too, this sight of the woods in moonlight, and the creek, smooth and faintly silver-colored, stretching out like a great wide path, and then sliding out of sight where it went into the darkness of a bend, that it should seem so familiar to me. As though I really knew where I was.

I sat there with my head sticking out from under the tarp, looking around at the moonlight and hearing the night sounds starting up again after the rain, the peepers peeping to each other and the frogs calling back and forth—rivet, rivet, it sounded like—and far down the creek a bullfrog starting up, with that slow deep gu-rump, and then a long wait, and then gu-rump again, as though he had all the time in the world. And for a time I wondered about it, about where I was and what I was doing and where I was going; and all I ended up with, that I was sure of, was that I was here, sitting in a boat tied to a tree somewhere on the western bank of the Little Star or Big Star Creek, waiting for morning; and what I was doing was looking for a lost skiff; and where I was going was yet to be seen. In a way, it didn't really seem strange at all. And then I went back in under the tarp. All right, I thought, maybe with Ellen off my mind now, tomorrow I can really get serious about looking for that skiff; it must be out there someplace. Finally, I went to sleep.

But the next morning, Jack seemed to have forgot all about the skiff we were supposed to be looking for; all he wanted to do was fish and fool around. He had come through the night just fine, he said, dry as a bone and sleeping like a log. This seemed to please him out of all proportion, as though it was some big victory over nature for him, which proved his cleverness to the world. It was a nuisance. No matter what I said, he would not take it seriously.

I had known from the way the day started that I was in for some nonsense; it was hardly daybreak, yet Jack was up and had unfastened the tarp and rolled it back, and when I opened my eyes I was looking up into the sky and Jack was standing there grinning down at me. "Another day, another opportunity," he said. Then before I was really awake good he had untied the boat and rowed us on down the creek to the clearing he had talked about, singing most of the way. What he sang was "Row, row, row your boat," and so forth, over and over, loud and off key, drowning out the birds. He seemed to like the last part of it best, because he would sort of shout it out, ". . . life is but a dream." It ruined what could have been one of the nicest parts of our trip yet, with the mist curling up off the water and the trees still wet and shining in the light of dawn, and the birds singing and fish jumping and all the sights and sounds of the woods seeming new and fresh again. Yet I couldn't really hold it against Jack; he was just that kind of a kid.

At the clearing Jack built a fire with some dead pitchy pine he found back in the woods and split up with the ax we had brought, and then he threw dead oak limbs on it to burn down and make coals we could cook on later. Then we rowed to the marsh grass across from the clearing, where we fished, using spinning rods and lures, for a solid hour or so, it seemed, with no luck at all. I was ready to give up on it after the first ten minutes. But Jack said we had to have fresh trout for breakfast, and he would try one lure after another, sure each time that the new lure would make the difference. I just kept casting out and reeling in, and when finally something gave my rod a jerk, I just sat there looking at the line pulled tight down toward the bottom of the creek thinking I had caught a snag. Then the line slacked up and not more than ten feet from the boat the water shot up and a big green-and-white fish shot up out of it and curled over and slapped back down and was gone from sight, trailing my line behind him. Jack gave a shout in my ear that startled me more than the fish had done. "Reel," he hollered, and I reeled and felt the line jerk again and then the fish fighting for his life with a kind of strength and fierceness that surprised me. But finally he seemed to tire, and when he came to the side of the boat and Jack slipped the net under him and got him into the boat, he just gave a few last flips and then lay there all tangled in the net, gulping at the air and heaving his sides, all his strength and struggle gone, as sad and yet as pretty a sight as you could see.

Jack just about jumped out of the boat with excitement. "He is three pounds if he's an ounce," he said, "three pounds if he's an ounce." He kept saying it over, and giving me a punch on the arm and then a clap on the back, and then just slapping his own two hands together, wham; so as not to hurt anybody, I guess. "We have got our fish for breakfast and then some," he said, "thanks to your beginner's luck." Then he went back to fishing as though he never meant to quit.

It was my bad luck to have been the one to catch the fish instead of Jack, as for the next hour more, it seemed, I sat there getting chewed up by the mosquitoes, which had got bad for some reason after the rain, hoping Jack would finally catch a fish himself and get even, so that we could go in and have some food. I was starved.

It was a bass that I had caught. Jack called it a green trout, and when I said that it looked like a bass to me, he said that was what a bass was, a green trout, although I believed it was right the other way around. By the time Jack was willing to quit on trying to catch us another one, my own poor fish had long ago given one last flop and died. So we rowed back to the clearing, and with a lot of unnecessary advice from Jack I cleaned the fish while he built the fire back up, and then Jack cooked it in the big iron skillet we had brought, frying it in a ton of lard, deep-fat frying, he called it, although it looked to me more like the poor fish was being boiled in oil. Then we ate it, and even with the taste of lard, it had a sweet, wild, good taste to it that was new to me, as though all the natural taste was still in it, the way it might have tasted, maybe, if we had eaten it raw, although Jack had cooked it practically to a cinder.

But we had sure wasted a lot of time, which I finally pointed out to Jack. "It's nothing," he said. "What is our hurry? Why not enjoy ourselves some? The world will not stop if we do not find that skiff today. Or tomorrow, either. Or never. Why act so sad about it?"

"I am not sad," I said, "I am serious, is all; which sometimes I wish you could be for a change. After all, it was not you who lost the skiff, but me."

"All right," Jack said, "go ahead and spoil your own good time if you want to. For myself, if it was not for these mosquitoes, I would not have a worry in the world, so you will have to go on being serious by yourself."

Then we cleaned up our mess from breakfast and bailed the rain water out of the back of the boat and straightened it all up again, hanging the tarp up on the sapling that was still there between the two blackgum trees, to let it dry out for a while. After that we went swimming and washed and then just loafed around, with Jack fishing for bream for a while with grasshoppers for bait, with no luck at that, either. It must have been the middle of the morning at least before we got started back down the creek again. Jack wanted to row and I let him; claimed he needed the exercise.

We had put the canned foods and cooking stuff back in the front of the boat. Because the tarp was still wet, we had spread it out over everything there. "When people see it like that," Jack said, "they may figure we are hauling moonshine whiskey down the creek from our still hidden back in the woods. We could have some fun. If somebody at some landing asks us what we have got under that tarp, let me do the talking, as I look older than you, or more like a moonshiner anyhow. You try and look suspicious if you can. Or just keep looking serious; that will make them suspicious for sure."

I laughed. "Who would think two kids would be rowing down the creek with a load of whiskey?" I said.

"There is people," Jack said, "that will suspicion anything

if you give them half a chance. What I will say is, when they ask what is under that tarp, 'Oh that? Why I have just got that tarp spread out that way to dry.' Then I will go on telling them the truth and making it sound like a lie. Then we can just row away, leaving them to wonder about it. The people along the creek, the retired ones that have come from Mobile and elsewhere, nothing much happens in their lives at all; just the same wide creek going by, day after day, while they sit there watching it and getting old. By the time we get down to the basin, we could be practically famous up and down the river, just on suspicion."

"All right," I said, "I'll let you do the talking. And I will try not to laugh."

This seemed to please Jack, and he rowed along as though he was in a hurry now to get to some landings and see what would happen. The creek was growing wider and coming into fewer bends and longer straight stretches all the time. The bigger it got the more I wondered how a stream this wide and this deep could still be called a creek and not a river; it just didn't seem right. We stayed in near the west bank, and it was getting near noon when we came to the first landing. "Now," Jack said, "we are down on the Big Star at last."

It wasn't much of a landing, just a short little pier stuck out in the creek, with several busted planks in it, and one beat-up half-sunk old green boat tied up to it out at the end. If there was a house somewhere back in the woods behind it, I couldn't see it. "This may be the Big Star," I said, "but if this is civilization again, then you could have fooled me about it easy. One lousy half-sunk boat."

"Wait and see," Jack said, and then we eased around a big, wide bend, and on down the creek I could see all kinds of landings, with piers sticking way out into the creek and all kinds of boats tied to them, and here and there houses, built right down at the water's edge, a strange sight to see. There must have been eight or ten landings and maybe four or five houses, all in a bunch and right side by side. Then away farther down the creek, just before it reached another bend, I could see another bunch of landings. "Just around that bend," Jack said, "set back up on a little hill, about the only hill anywhere around here, is probably the oldest house on the creek. It is owned by Hank Byrd, who went to school with my pa. He's kind of strange, but Pa likes him. The quietest man you ever saw. While Mrs. Byrd, she is an experience. The way she talks, she hardly ever gets to finish a sentence before she has started another one. It's like listening to a tree full of birds. But if anyone knows something about Pa's lost skiff, he will be the one to have heard about it. People like to talk to him; he just listens."

Jack had been easing the boat in closer to the shore, and soon we came to the first of the landings. Back up from the pier I could see a house through the trees, but no people. There were three boats tied to the pier, none of them Mr. Haywood's. We went along from pier to pier, looking at all the boats. They were of all sorts and sizes, but none built at all like the one I had lost. Then up ahead we saw a man come out to the end of a pier and sit down on a bench that was there and sit looking up and down, out at the river. "See," Jack said, "he is sitting out in that hot sun like it was a natural thing to do, but the truth is he has been watching us and got suspicious. He cannot figure us out. Watch how his eyes bug out when he sees that tarp."

"Ask him about the skiff," I said.

"I will," Jack said, "but he will think it's a lie."

"I wish you would get serious," I said.

"Just think about all that moonshine whiskey we have got hid under the tarp," Jack said. "And watch me sneak by him." I gave up and sat back and watched down the creek. The whole thing had got me somehow nervous. When Jack is being a clown there is no arguing with him.

Then we moved on along and came to the pier with the man sitting on it, with Jack looking up and down the creek and around behind him and everywhere but at the man, who sat there staring down at us. Whether or not he was staring at the tarp I couldn't tell. I tried not to look at him. "Are you boys looking for something?" the man said. It embarrassed me, the way we hadn't even said hello

Jack jerked his head up and stopped rowing, easing the front of the boat around so the man could get a good look at it, and then swinging it on around like he was trying to hide it. "Why, no, not exactly," Jack said. "We are just on our way down the creek."

"Not exactly?" the man said.

"Well," Jack said, "some time ago we had an old cypress skiff go adrift, but we have about give up on ever finding it again."

"Is that so," the man said.

"Yes, sir," Jack said. "But it is nothing to bother about."

"You're from up the creek?" the man said.

"Not exactly," Jack said. "Although that is the way we have come. It has sure got hot today, ain't it?" We were drifting away from the pier, I noticed, and Jack let it drift. I looked up at the man and I could see he was not satisfied about us at all.

"It is a plain old cypress skiff," I said, "pointed at both ends. I was the one that lost it. I'm from White Plains, New York. Have you seen such a boat?"

The man stood up then, still puzzled, I guess, but we were drifting farther away. "No," he said, "but if you have come that far, I certainly hope you find it." Then he laughed and shook his head and went back up the pier toward his house.

"You ruined it," Jack said. "Just when I had him all confused. Did you notice the way he kept looking at that tarp?"

"Jack," I said, "all I saw him looking at was you. Like he thought you were a nut. And he was right. Now maybe we can just keep looking for the skiff."

After that, Jack decided that it was time for me to row. I was glad to do it. I felt like I could use some exercise myself, and the hurt of the blisters on my hands gave me something sensible to worry about for a change.

At the next bunch of landings it was the same, all sorts of boats, big and small, but none of them Mr. Haywood's skiff. And no one even came down to see what Jack was trying to act so suspicious about. "It is the wrong time of day," Jack said.

102

"In this heat, they would probably not get too curious if we was both acting drunk as well as suspicious."

"All I am interested in," I said, "is finding your father's skiff. And so far, I haven't seen one even built the same." It was discouraging. The sight of all those boats had got my hopes up. For some reason or other, the way things had happened, I was more and more determined to find that skiff if it could be found. But it was clear that Jack hardly cared.

"It's time we got out of this heat and had something to eat," Jack said. "That last broken-down pier up ahead has not been used in years. If it's still safe to stand on, we can tie up there. That crazy roof they have over it out at the end is full of holes, but it will do for shade. I have fished from it often. Never caught a thing."

When we got to it I could see it was in bad shape all right, with a number of pilings rotted clear through at the water line and just hanging there, and with planks broken out and rotted through all over it. Yet the shade looked good. So we tried it, and while it shook a lot at first, it didn't fall down, even when Jack jumped up and down a couple of times to see if it would. Somehow I was not especially hungry, not for cold collard greens or Polish sausage and crackers again, anyhow, which was what Jack ate. Then he got a cigar and smoked it, stretched out on his back looking up at the holes in the roof and resting, he said. I would have sooner put up with the mosquitoes, or just kept going. But Jack claimed he was satisfied where he was. So we stayed there for what seemed a couple of hours, although it was probably not that long, with nothing for me to do but look out at the creek and watch a few motorboats go by near the other shore, so far away they looked like toys, with the sound of their motors trailing away behind them, like echoes, it seemed. Then later I watched a single fish, out in the middle of the creek, heading upstream and half the time in the air in some of the laziest, easiest jumps you could imagine, sort of sliding up out of the water and hanging there stretched out like he was trying sailing for a ways, level with the creek and then flopping back in on his belly with a kind of soft hollow sound that hardly sounded like the noise of a jumping fish at all. I would see the water falling away and then his white belly flashing in the sun and then down he would come again, and then the easy plop he made would come drifting across the water to me in the hot, quiet air. I thought maybe Jack had gone to sleep, but without rolling over to look and make sure he said, "That's a mullet you are watching. They just love to jump."

I watched it jumping on up the creek until it was out of sight. "Seems to me," I said, "that a mullet, if that is what it was, must have a better reason for jumping than that."

"If he does," Jack said, "nobody knows it. And I would not have said it was a mullet if it wasn't. Of course if you would like to believe that it is the shrimp grass tickling their stomachs that makes them jump, or that they like to whop down on their bellies to get rid of gas, or that they just want to see up ahead where the creek is going, you can take your pick and believe what you want. I have heard all such things and more being guessed at. But Ma's guess is that they jump for joy. Ma is a great believer in the natural joy of wild things; right up to the minute that they may be caught and ate by something else. Which is something I wouldn't know about for sure; but I suspect that in the case of why mullet jump, she may be right."

To be honest, I had never thought too much about such things one way or another. I have often wondered why people do some of the things they do, but the world of nature seemed to me something that you could take for granted. A fish jumps, so to speak, because he jumps. But I didn't argue it with Jack; after all, it was me who had brought the question up.

Then Jack jumped up and set the pier to shaking, although just what made *him* jump up like that for no good reason was something I didn't bother to ask. "We are wasting time," he said, "we cannot just lie around here watching mullet jump all day."

Whatever it was that had got into him, I was glad to see him ready to get on down the creek again. "You're right," I said, "it's time to get on down to where there are some more landings, as that is most likely where we will finally find the skiff. How far is it before we come on some more?"

"Except for Hank Byrd's place," he said, "quite a ways." Then we got back into the boat and started off again, Jack rowing and moving us right along. The creek ran straight for a time and then we came to the bend, and it was the longest and slowest bend we had come to yet. It kept curving back around, slow but steady. "Just before we get to Byrd's landing," Jack said, "there is a bream hole Pa has told me about that I have never looked into. It is back off the creek in a kind of slough, and you cannot get into it for the mud flat at its mouth except at high water, which we still will have when we get there if I keep rowing good. Pa says it is full of water lilies and grass; but that with patience, the biggest goggle-eyes on the creek can be caught there. You will notice an odd thing when we get to Byrd's landing; while it is on the west bank of the creek, it also looks out west. Right at this point, the creek has doubled back on itself."

"Actually," I said, "I am more interested in finding your father's skiff than in fishing for bream, but if you want to spend a few minutes back in this slough I guess we could give it a try."

"Goggle-eyes," Jack said, "is just about the sweetest-tasting fish there is." The creek kept curving back around, getting wider as it went, and Jack kept rowing, watching the shore close. Even so, we almost went past the place he was watching for. It was just a small opening in the trees, coming in on a slant the same way the creek was curving, so that you had to go almost past it before you could see it. Mostly, it looked like a small stretch of marsh. But when we came in close to it, we could see it opening out, back through the trees, with stretches of clear water here and there, but thick with water lilies, too, yellow ones, and a surprising sight to see. "This is it, all right," Jack said, and he rowed straight on toward it through the marsh grass. And I thought we had made it, and so did he, when the boat gave a lurch and dragged on a bit and then came to a stop.

Jack stood up and looked down into the water, first at the

105

back of the boat and then the front. "We have went aground," he said, "in mud. We are still somewhat overloaded at the back, and that is where we are caught. But I believe we can get on through this muck, if we work it right."

"Maybe we can try it on the way back," I said. "The tide already seems to be going out, and if we do get in there, there is the business of getting back out again later."

"Coming back we will be on the other side of the creek," Jack said, "and the tide is not going out all that fast. We could just look around at least. I'll get out in back and try pushing." So he jumped out the back, and the mud seemed to hold him up better than I thought it would, but all his pushing and rocking the boat hardly moved us a foot. "You get up in front," Jack said finally, wiping sweat off his face. "The front end is clear; it is just the last few inches of the back that is stuck." He waited and I went up to the front, stumbling over the things under the tarp, and then I sat right at the end and leaned back while he grunted and shoved away and even cussed some, but we still stayed stuck.

"It's no use," I said. "Stay where you are and pull, and I will jump off and push from this end and we will get back to looking for the skiff, which is what we are supposed to be doing anyhow."

"Rodney," Jack said, acting a little sore, "I swear you are the quickest to give up on a thing that I have ever seen."

Which was a lie. "All right," I said, "I will come back and help you push, and if we end up spending the night in that slough getting eaten up by mosquitoes, I can take it if you can."

"It is not more pushing we need," Jack said. "I can push all right. What we need is some real brains about this. Look, I am some forty pounds heavier than you. If I get up there where you are, it will bring the back end that much higher. If you can come back here and find the strength to give one good shove, I believe we will float clear."

It was all right with me and I said so. "I will lift *and* shove," I said. "Speaking of brains."

"Just shove," Jack said. "My weight should do the rest." So

106

we changed places and I got back and sank down in the muck up to my knees and set myself, grabbing the boat under the bottom and getting ready to heave and push when Jack gave the word. I could just see him over the edge of the back, I was so low. He was standing up on the very end of the front, at the edge of the little seat there. "I will jump up and come down," Jack said, "and when you feel the back end come up, give a shove like your skinny butt had just caught fire."

I was pretty mad by this time about the whole damn foolishness; so I braced myself. "Jump when you are ready," I said. "Only try to come down on the boat." Then Jack yelled, "Now!" and I jerked up on the bottom of the boat and gave it a shove with all the strength I had. It shot out from under me like a feather, and I went down on my face in the swamp grass and muck, but we were clear.

When I got back up, the boat had drifted off into a bunch of lilies, and Jack was nowhere in sight. "Jack?" I hollered. Then slowly his head came up into sight from the bottom of the boat. Even that far off I could see how white it was. He held one hand up, held by the arm with his other hand, sort of showing it to me. "Are you hurt?" I said.

Jack shook his head, and then in the faintest voice I had ever heard him use, he said, "Not much. But, Rodney, I have broke my wrist."

10

For a minute I stood there, knee deep in mud, staring at Jack
sitting in the bottom of the boat in the middle of the yellow
water lilies, still holding his hand up for me to see, his face a
kind of dirty grey. Then I jerked myself loose and half waded
and half swam to the boat, pushing lilies out of my way and
stumbling around, but getting there faster than I thought I
could. Then I was up in the boat looking down at Jack, and it
was clear from the way he sat there, staring at his wrist, that
he was in pain and no doubt of it. "Does it hurt much?" I
said.

"I can stand it," Jack said. "But I heard it break. It went
snap. Just like a stick. I heard it."

"Just stay there," I said. "I will get us out of here and down
to Byrd's landing; and if they have a phone we will call your
father, or else I will find some place where there is a phone.
This is serious."

Then Jack, still sitting there pale and hurt-looking, tried to
smile. "You do like a thing to be serious," he said. "But maybe
this time you are right. It is broke for sure. See, I cannot even
wiggle my fingers."

"It was my fault," I said. "I shoved too hard. But you just
sit there and I'll get us out of here in a hurry." Then I
jumped back out of the boat to make it lighter, and got
around at the back and pushed it over to the mud flat. Then I
went around to the front and found the track we had made in
the mud coming in, and I got the boat pointed toward it and
worked my way around to the back and backed off and then
made a run for it, as best I could, and we dragged a little, but
we went over the mud and out into the creek.

"You done that good," Jack said.

108

"Don't you worry," I said, jumping up into the boat, "I will get you there in a hurry," and then I started rowing, as fast as I could. Rowing, I turned and looked at Jack. He looked awful. "Is it hurting worse?" I said.

Jack shook his head no. "But I have went and acted the fool for sure," he said.

"I'll find a phone somewhere and call The Hill," I said. "It's my fault for losing your father's skiff in the first place. And I am sorry about the way it must be hurting. I am rowing as fast as I can."

How he did it I don't know, but Jack actually laughed. It was faint and quick, but it was a laugh. "I swear," Jack said, "if the world was to end tomorrow, you would somehow manage to die believing it was all your fault. Actually, I see I can move my fingers a bit now if I really try. They was probably only paralyzed from the shock. It could just be a sprain after all."

I didn't argue with him. If it was just a sprain, I figured, why was he still just sitting there where he had fallen, still so pale that the dirt on his face stood out in splotches, and holding his hurt arm in a grip so tight that all his fingernails were white, like he was trying to shut out the pain? If it had of been anyone else, they would have been crying. I was half close to it myself; at the way he tried to hide it. "Just hang on," I said. "Maybe if Mr. Byrd has a car he will be willing to drive you back to The Hill himself and save the time."

Jack looked at me and shook his head, and then eased up off the bottom of the boat and kicked his way through the stuff under the tarp and crawled past me until he could sit down on the back seat. "I am not dying," he said, "or even hurting more than I can stand. I have only lamed my wrist. You are getting us in too close to the bank; pull more on your left."

It was guts, and I had to admire it. "Keep telling me which way to pull," I said, "and I will row." Then I leaned into it even more than I had been doing already, and the sweat rolled down off me, but we moved along in a way that Jack noticed, despite his pain.

"There is no need to kill yourself," he said, "we are almost there. More on your right now. It is starting to hurt more like a sprain all the time. It was that stupid tarp I left spread out like that to fool people. I could not see where I was falling. Once, I sprained my ankle so bad I could not wiggle my toes."

"Keep me headed toward the landing," I said. I was blinking sweat out of my eyes and could not really see, but I kept rowing. That was all there was I could do.

"First cold water and then hot, that was all Ma used," Jack said, "and by morning the worst of the pain and some of the swelling was gone. The Byrds will have some hot and cold water for sure."

"You do not fix a broken wrist with hot and cold water," I said. "What you need is a doctor. And that is what we will get. Am I headed right?"

"Dead on it," Jack said. He was quiet for a while, while I rowed, and then I saw him look at his wrist again and shake his head. "Rodney," he said, "the way it hurts, it may be broke at that. If I have ruined your trip, I sure am sorry." Then he hung down his head for the first time. I turned and looked behind me, and there was the landing, well in view, but still far off. I kept my own head down and rowed. Then after a while Jack said, "A little on your left now; you're doing fine." I looked at him, and he was still as white as he had been since he fell, and he was still holding his arm out up in front of him, but not so tight, and he had tried to get comfortable on the seat, leaning back a little. He was watching up ahead somewhat in the same way I remembered him when we had started out, leaning back then and smoking a cheap cigar, looking out at the creek like he was king of the world. "It may just be a sprain," he said. "There is no way of telling from the pain. One can hurt as bad as the other, I believe. You can start easing off; we are almost there."

I slowed down some, and then Jack sat up again and said, "On your right now," and then, "Steady," and then, "On your left a little," and finally he said, "Okay, Rodney, just let it coast." And I did, wiping the sweat from my eyes, and seeing the shore up close out of the corner of my eye and waiting for the boat to bump up against the pier, too tired to turn and stop it, seeing Jack looking up and nodding to himself like we were coming in fine.

Then as though we had run up on another mudbank, the boat gave an easy lurch and slowed and stopped, and, surprised, I turned, and on the front end of the boat, holding it, was a small, bare, brown sort of foot that I somehow knew was a girl's. Then tired and worried as I was, I turned more and stared at the long, smooth stuck-down leg, amazed, as though I couldn't believe it, and then finally like some kind of an idiot I raised my head and saw who it was, and she was a girl, all right, wearing white shorts and a yellow blouse, hanging out over the water holding onto a post, still holding our boat with her toes and looking down at me, with long brown hair hanging down around the most serious, wondering, beautiful face you could imagine; as surprised as I was, I guess, to meet like this, so close and unexpected, and strangers. I just stared at her; and she stared back. "The fast way you were rowing," she said, "I was afraid someone was hurt. Is it Jack?"

"He has broken his wrist," I said. "It was my fault. I'm his friend, Rodney Blankhard."

For a second or so more we still stared at each other, still serious, caught by surprise, it seemed, and then she smiled, as shy and yet as pretty as could be, half like a kid, but like a girl who knows she is not just a kid, either, and holds back a little. "I am pleased to meet you," she said. "I am Brenda Sue Byrd."

How Jack could have told me all about her father and mother and said not a word about a girl like Brenda Sue Byrd was what finally amazed me most of all. For a time, it had just about made me forget about Jack's broken wrist altogether. Then I remembered what I was doing and grabbed a post and swung up onto the pier and tied up the front of the boat, while Brenda Sue pulled in the back end so Jack could get out, talking to him like an old friend, which I guess he was, asking him how much did it hurt and how did he do it, and was he sure it was broken.

"Broke or bad sprained," Jack said. "But it is nothing to make a big fuss about."

111

"The way your friend was rowing," Brenda Sue said, "nobody rows that hard just for fun. But when I saw it was you in the back, I thought maybe you had made some crazy kind of bet with him. When you got close and didn't even say hello, though, I was near to certain that something was wrong. Pa has the car torn up, fixing it, but we could call your pa to come get you if you want."

I was glad to know they had a telephone. Jack just stood there on the pier, back in the shade under the roof, showing off his wrist to Brenda Sue and even smiling about it, much as it must have hurt, as though it was practically something to be proud of. He seemed in no hurry about it at all, now we had got here. "Jack said he heard it snap," I said, "and I believe him. I shoved the boat clean out from under him and then fell on my face myself, so I didn't hear it. Anyhow, Jack is no doctor and neither am I, and a doctor is the one who will say if it is sprained or broken. So if it is not too much trouble I think we should call Mr. Haywood right away."

"Rodney," Jack said, "if it was you that broke my wrist like you claim, then the least you could do was to let me be the one to decide what to do about it." Then he turned to Brenda Sue. "Only it was me that done it, being a fool." He made it sound like bragging.

She nodded, not needing to be convinced, it seemed, and this pleased me more than I should have let it right then; and when she answered him, it was actually me that she turned and talked to. "Maybe we should go up to the house and see what my folks think about it," she said. "You are right; if Jack has really broke his wrist his pa had best come get him."

"Listen," Jack said, "instead of all this talk about it, what I would most like to do is get this wrist laid down in a basin of ice-cold water. Then we can talk. But there is no big rush about calling Pa. I am not in danger, just in pain."

Jack was right about not just standing there, anyhow, and I knew it and was sorry, because hard as I kept trying to worry about his wrist, I was still more willing to stand there talking to Brenda Sue and watching her, not really in a hurry at all to see what could be done to ease Jack's pain. Actually, instead of feeling bad about Jack, like I should have been, I had already got around to feeling bad about his sister, as though just that quick and with no struggle against it, I had let this girl I didn't even know yet push the picture of Ellen right out of my mind. I was hardly acting normal. Surprises, I thought; now I am even surprising myself. "Jack is right," I said, "the first thing he needs is some help from the pain, if we can get it."

"To start with," Jack said, "some good cold water would be fine; for my wrist, and to drink as well." So we all went walking slow, to stay with Jack, up the long path to the house, with Jack talking a little, mostly to himself, arguing that what he probably had was only a sprain after all, as he was finding he could wiggle his fingers more all the time. Then we went up the steps and on into a big screened-in porch, where Mrs. Byrd was waiting for us, having the same big bright-brown eyes and long brown hair and generally dark complexion that Brenda Sue had, but being maybe a good hundred pounds or more heavier. So we told her about Jack's wrist, and he held it out for her to see, saying once again that it was probably only sprained. To my surprise, she hardly glanced at it, but put her head on one side and sort of stared Jack in the eye for a minute, and then she said, "Why, Jack Haywood, of course it is broke and you know it." Then she turned to Brenda Sue. "Babe Honey," she said, "go out back and get your pa from under the car and tell him to come look at this boy. Jack, you sit down on that chair there and let your head hang down and get some blood up in it, before you go altogether faint and fall and bust your other arm. I'll get some water for you."

Then she left, and for a minute there was only Jack and me on the porch, Jack sitting in the chair like she had told him to, hanging his head down, while I stood there in front of him, not knowing of a thing I could do. Then without lifting up his head Jack said, "Rodney, if you let them call Pa, and he comes up here, that will be the end of your trip as well as mine. He will not let you go on down that creek and back up it all alone. He would be wrong, in my opinion. I believe you could do it without trouble. But I know Pa. That's why I am arguing that all I have is a sprain. To get some time. I believe I can work something out, if you will only keep your mouth shut for a while. This wrist is broke and I know it, just like Mrs. Byrd said. But she can't prove it. And for as long as I go on saying it's a sprain, you try acting like you believe it for a change." Then he lifted his head to see if I understood him; I was surprised at how he had got his color back. He even gave me that sly grin he gets when he thinks he has noticed something. "If I can stand the pain," he said, "seems you could stand the company awhile. Was you surprised when you seen her?"

I just shook my head at him. "Jack," I said, "I stay surprised."

Then Mrs. Byrd came out with a basin of water with ice floating in it and put it on the table next to Jack's chair and he eased his wrist down into it. Then she came back with some water to drink, and then sat there asking both of us questions faster than either of us could answer, about our trip and the skiff we were looking for and how the people all were on The Hill, as though having done what could be done about Jack's wrist, we all might as well sit back and enjoy our visit. Then Mr. Byrd came in, a short man, wearing dirty overalls and no shoes, but with a straight, friendly way of looking at you. He shook Jack's hand—it was the left wrist that Jack had broken —and then mine, when Jack told him who I was. And then he looked at Jack's wrist, and said quietly, "Can you move it, Jack?"

"I believe I could if it wasn't for the pain," Jack said. "I would sooner wait to prove it, though."

"Why, Hank," Mrs. Byrd said, "you can see in his eyes that it's broke. He's just afraid to shame himself before his pa."

Mr. Byrd sort of cleared his throat, as though what his wife had said had embarrassed him. "If it is broke, Jack," he said, "I believe your pa would not appreciate it if we failed to let him know. But it is up to you, of course."

"It has only just happened," Jack said. "I would rather wait awhile and see, if it would not inconvenience you too much. I would hate to have my pa have to come haul me back to The

Hill this evening for only a swollen sprain that may have started going back down by morning."

Mr. Byrd nodded, as though what Jack had said seemed reasonable to him, as it even did to me, even though I knew better. Still, I thought I ought to try and help Jack out, if that was what he wanted. "I'm sure sorry that we have put you to all this trouble," I said, "but a few days ago I went off alone in Mr. Haywood's cypress skiff, the one he built himself. And I let it drift off and lost it. We have been looking for it since. That is what we were doing when Jack sprained his wrist, looking for it back in a slough where it might have drifted." For me, this was a pretty good bit of straightforward lying. But Mr. Byrd looked at me and nodded the same as he had with Jack.

"It's no trouble at all," he said. "I know the skiff. Just yesterday there was a party with three boats, put up at the point, down in the basin, with one of the boats a cypress skiff. They had set up a camp, so it is possible they might still be there."

"Then we cannot quit now," Jack said. "This is the first we have even heard of a skiff like Pa's since we left The Hill."

"You are welcome to stay, of course," Mrs. Byrd said, "and if finding that skiff means so much to you both, I guess we can wait and see how Jack makes up his mind about his wrist. But I am not going to let you put it in hot water, too, Jack, the way you said. Because that is only right for sprains. Babe Honey, why don't you get some more ice for Jack. In this heat, it lasts no time at all."

"Ice alone will be fine." Jack said. Then Mr. Byrd went back to working on his car, and Mrs. Byrd went back into the kitchen, and before Brenda Sue got back with the ice, Jack said, "If I can hold out until morning, I have a plan so that you can go on by yourself if you want to."

"Jack," I said, "I would just hate to go back to The Hill with one more thing gone wrong and gone wrong on account of me, if not because of me, and not having even finished the job of looking for the skiff I lost. But if you have got to sit here all night long with your arm stuck down in that ice, just

115

to gain me the time, then I think you should let me call your pa to come and get us now."

Jack shook his head. "It don't hurt all that bad," he said, "and I imagine it would hurt as much back home on The Hill as it probably will here."

"But if it's a broken bone, what if it sets up crooked?"

"It will hardly set itself overnight," Jack said. "I will tell you my plan when no one is around. It is simple, but sure to work. In the meantime you can visit with Brenda Sue Babe Honey Byrd. Ain't that a lot of name, though? Here she comes now."

Then for a while there was just the three of us sitting there on the porch, looking out from the western bank of Big Star Creek and yet watching the sun setting in the west, with everything else seeming just as strange and turned around to me, and with none of us being able to think of much to talk about at all. With Jack, it was mostly a matter of the pain, I guess. With Brenda Sue, it was probably the fact of Jack's trouble and unusual quietness, and that I was still so much a stranger. With me, it was the simple matter of Brenda Sue Babe Honey Byrd.

11

I spent the rest of the evening after supper worrying about Jack and wondering about Brenda Sue. I had never known anyone quite like her before; she was the most shy and yet the most open in her manner of any girl I had met. I cannot describe it, but when she looked at you, she *looked* at you; yet she would look down when she talked sometimes, and talk so soft I could hardly hear her. Her own smile would somehow seem to embarrass her, and she would stop it almost as soon as it had got started, so mostly it was just a kind of quick start of a smile, and then it would be gone; but in that second or so the difference would be like night and day, as though her whole face had been lit by a glow. As dark as she was and as serious-looking most of the time, this was something to see. Toward the end of the evening it had got to be something I was watching for. Even so, it always somehow surprised me.

Yet shy as she was at first, about talking and about her smile, Brenda Sue did not bother to pretend to anyone, including me, that she had not somehow found me interesting, right from the start. The truth is, just about every time I looked at her I would discover she was already looking at me. It was a new experience, and somewhat embarrassing at first. But she acted so natural about it that I finally started feeling more natural when I looked at her, and this had never happened so easy with me with a girl before. There was such a friendly, serious thing in her expression, when she wasn't smiling or trying not to smile, that only an ape could have misunderstood it. She was interested, and wondered who I was. And I wondered back.

I would be lying if I tried to say that all I had noticed about Brenda Sue was her serious expression and her smile. To begin with, the very first sight I had got of her was only of her leg. For so short a girl, it had seemed at the time one of the longest, smoothest legs I had ever seen. And, naturally, she had another just like it. In the white shorts she was wearing, and as well tanned as she was, when Brenda Sue walked, anywhere, it was something you noticed. She stepped right out, too. And when she stood up, she stood up straight. She had no shyness about her figure, anyhow, which I would say was just about perfect. Another thing I had noticed, and while it may seem a strange thing to say of a girl, you just knew she had muscles. I don't mean big muscles that you could see, but there was this neatness about her, a firmness, I guess, with no slack anywhere, so to speak; maybe just a healthiness. But you noticed it. I guess what seemed most unusual to me, although it is not the fault of other girls but my fault for thinking along such lines, but Brenda Sue did not strike my mind the way most other girls have been apt to do, as either a pretty face, or bouncy breasts, or a fanny that moves nice, or legs I would like to see more of, or as *only* one thing or another; she seemed altogether special, all of her. Which is probably as honest as I ought to get about it. But it was not just her shyness or smile that I had noticed; not at all.

And whatever she noticed and may have wondered about me, I believe she remembered well enough that I had not come riding up to her house on a big white horse, a knight in shining armor, but rowing my head off, scared and half covered with mud, a more or less normal kid, who, the first thing he did when he saw her, was to sit there staring at her long bare leg, for all the world as though he might have liked to bite it.

With her shyness and soft way of talking, I have not meant to make it seem that Brenda Sue struck me as being nothing but a nice sort of backward kid. I mean that when I would glance over and see her sitting there looking at me, it would not be like a fool, but like a girl. Yet she was not being cute about it, either; just open. Like right after we had eaten supper and I went down to straighten up the boat before it got too dark; I didn't ask her if she would like to come along or anything, in fact it was Jack who I told where I was going, but when I left, Brenda Sue got up and just came along with me, not saying a word, walking beside me down the long curving path to the pier as though it was nothing more or less than I had expected. Then she sat there at the edge of the pier in the last of the sunlight swinging her legs out over the water and watching me straighten up the stuff in the boat and cover it up with the tarp for the night. Looking down like that, I guess she saw a lot of my hair, because finally, having first said something about how well supplied with food we were, she said, as naturally as though she might have been mentioning the sunset or something, "You sure do have nice hair." Just that. And when I looked up at her, surprised, she was not even smiling, just sitting there swinging her legs and looking as serious about it as if she had mentioned something sad. All I could do was wonder.

Then I went back to working at the boat. "Well," I said, "these stupid curls of mine have brought me more trouble than any other single thing." And then thinking I might be misunderstood altogether, I was quick to say, "From boys. But there is nothing I can do about it."

"I like curls," she said. Then she let it go at that, and so did I.

When I had finished with the stuff in the boat, I got up and sat at the edge of the pier beside her for a while, watching the sunset, trying to get my mind back on Jack, still wondering if I was doing the right thing in not calling his father to come get him, letting him sit up there with a broken wrist for as long as I already had, just so I could keep my word about looking for the skiff. While in the meantime I could also sit here, watching the light lifting up off the creek, with Brenda Sue, who I hadn't even asked, sitting beside me, swinging her legs out now and then where I could see them, both in the air and reflected in the water, a pretty sight to see. It just didn't seem right or fair to Jack.

Still, we sat there together, watching the sunset and talking, until there wasn't any sunset left to see. She had, she told me when I asked her, just turned fifteen. The soft way she said it,

119

it was as though it still seemed a kind of wonder to her. It somehow did to me, anyhow. I had said I was almost sixteen. Or maybe it just seemed a kind of wonder to us both, to be not altogether strangers any more, although strangers so short a time ago, and to be just the ages that we were, and to be sitting there together, alone, talking in the dark.

For a while after that we just sat there, and finally I said, "I guess I had better go see how poor Jack is coming along," and I got up and Brenda Sue got up and we walked back up the hill toward the house together, finally coming into the light again, and turning at the same time to look at each other, each of us caught, wondering and surprised, it seemed, and then pleased, I guess. Anyhow, I must have smiled, because Brenda Sue did, and it held this time, long. And when she finally ducked her head, it seemed to me that for the time her smile had held I must have also held my breath. For a second after, anyhow, I was left half dizzy; and if that seems half crazy, it is still the truth. Then we went on up the path and up onto the porch and looked at Jack.

He was sitting there in a chair with his left hand stuck inside his shirt, with a big Sears, Roebuck catalogue on the table in front of him spread open to a double page of guns, pretending he was reading about them. He hardly lifted up his head when we came in together. He looked terrible. "Why have you got your hand inside your shirt? Has the swelling gone down any?" I said.

"Because I am tired of trying to freeze it plum off," Jack said, "and I don't have a sling for it. Even with only a sprain, a sling can help. Brenda Sue, your ma says for you to do the dishes. She is out back with your pa at the car, holding a light for him."

"I will fix you a decent sling first," Brenda Sue said, and she ran off the porch and came back with a big, thin red scarf and went around behind Jack's chair and leaned over him, ready to fix his sling, but Jack wouldn't take his hand back out of his shirt so that she could adjust it.

"Just tie the two ends together like you've got it now," he

said, "and if it needs adjusting Rodney can do it while you are washing up the dishes." It hardly sounded friendly, but she guessed at it and did it the best she could, and then went back into the kitchen. But when Jack had eased his hand back out of his shirt and into the sling, I could see what he had been doing; he had not wanted her to see it. It was swollen to at least twice its normal size. "You know what I think?" Jack said. "I believe I have broke *and* badly sprained my wrist, both."

I stood there looking at him, feeling like hell about it. "Damn it," I said, "it is time to stop this craziness and call your father."

"No it's not," Jack said, "not after what I have went through already."

"Jack," I said, "I can see how much it has swollen and I can guess at how much it must hurt. Being stubborn about it just doesn't make sense. We can look for that skiff another time. No matter what I have said before, it is not that important to me."

"Just wait," Jack said, "this sling is really giving me the first relief I have had. Anyhow, Rodney, when you have made up your mind about a thing, you should let it stay made up for a time. Or people will get not to trust your word."

I stood looking down at him, shaking my head and not really knowing what to say, and finally I said, "It may seem strange to you, or a sign of weakness, but I do not like to see people suffer. Whether from my stupidity or their own."

"Honest, Rodney," he said, "I am not really suffering all that much. Look, here is how we will do it. I have asked Mrs. Byrd and we can sleep here on the porch; there are some cots around on the other side. I will get you up early. Then I will claim to the Byrds that my wrist is better, only not quite well enough yet so that I can be of help to you going on down to the basin. Then I will say, 'But there is no reason Rodney should not go on down to the basin and get that skiff by himself. If he rows like I know he can row, he can get down there and back, easy, by early evening.' And by then my wrist

121

will be rested enough and we can make it back up the creek, just taking our time, and still get back up to The Landing on Saturday!"

"By Saturday," I said, "your broken bone may have started setting up crooked, and there is no way for you to sleep comfortable with a broken wrist either in the boat or in the woods, and rains may come up and hold us back. And all that time your wrist will be hurting like hell and nothing will have been done about it; and your lousy plan is no plan at all. It's crazy."

But Jack shook his head for a bit, as though I was the crazy one. "You have not let me finish," he said. "Naturally I would not wait and let you take forever rowing us both back up the creek. You have not thought it out. What I will do, once you get good and started down the creek tomorrow, I will discover that my wrist is surely broke after all. Then I'll call Pa. And when he gets here, if he wants to wait for you to get back from the basin, I will be in such pain as to make a wait seem cruel. And he will have to take me back to get this bone set. Then you can go on and look as much as you please for the skiff, just so you manage to get back to The Landing by Saturday. Which I believe you can manage to do." He looked at me and waited, and when I still couldn't think of what to say, he said, "Well, that's my plan. And unless you are actually afraid of a few nights alone on the creek, then you have got no reason to talk about calling Pa. I will do it in the morning."

I just stood there looking at him, and then finally I gave up on it. "No," I said, "I don't know any more what is right, but I'm not afraid of the creek alone. I will do it. But if you have the sense to change your mind before morning, I hope you will have the nerve to admit it. It's good to be brave, I guess, but there is nothing wrong about having good sense, either."

Then I looked up and saw Brenda Sue standing in the door to the porch right off behind us. How long she had been standing there I could only wonder; at least for a while, I figured. Jack saw me staring and turned enough to see her. And then the first one of us to think of something to say was

122

Brenda Sue. "Ma called in for me to come ask how your wrist was feeling now," she said.

"Tell your ma, thank you," Jack said, "I believe it's feeling better."

For a time longer Brenda Sue stood there, looking first to Jack and then to me, and then looking last at me, she said, "If that's what you want, that's what I will tell her." I just nodded, and she left. Then in no time she was back, and she went around in back of Jack and untied his sling and pulled it up some and then tied it again. "The least you can do with that wrist," she said, "is have it held right." And then we sat there, with Jack gone back to reading the catalogue and Brenda Sue and me sitting there talking about other things, with the light from the moon finally showing clear on the clearing and the creek below.

Finally Mr. and Mrs. Byrd came in, tired from working on the car, but pleased that it was done and running again. Jack had to do some good arguing, even interrupting Mrs. Byrd several times, to get her to change her mind about their driving us both back to The Hill right then. The way he finally won was to act like he was getting his feelings hurt at their being in such a hurry to get rid of us, even though we had been there since shortly after noon. "Well," Jack said finally, "for some reason Ellen and the folks could not seem to wait to run me and Rodney back off to the creek, but I guess I can see why you should not want us just hanging around here, either. I am sure sorry for the trouble we have put you to already, as well as the trouble now of that long drive back to The Hill, but that is up to you, of course. Rodney and me can come look around in the basin for that skiff some other time, although I imagine it will be gone by then for sure."

Then he hung his head and shook it a bit from side to side, as though he had just been told he had not a friend left in the world. It was the worst I had seen him act yet, but it worked. "Jack Haywood," Mrs. Byrd said, "you know very well that you and your friend Rodney are more than welcome to spend the night here, as I have already said. It is not a question of

123

that at all, and I am surprised that you could think such a thing. I'll have Babe Honey make up the cots for you right away. It was only your wrist we were thinking about. Why, all this time we have been talking, I have never seen a boy looking more worried about his friend than Rodney there worrying about you. And I am worried, too. But we can wait until morning, if that is still what you want to do."

I had been worried about Jack's wrist all along, but at the time Mrs. Byrd had been watching me I had been worried most of all about Jack's lying and his lousy job of acting like he had had his feelings hurt. In a way, if they had thrown us both out on our heads after that I would not have blamed them; still, I had to admit that when Jack gets his mind set on something he will not let it easily be changed.

Then Brenda Sue went away and came back with her arms loaded down with sheets and bedding and pillows, and I jumped up to help her. It seemed the least I could do, although I could see it surprised them all at first. To be honest, after we went around to the other side of the porch, just Brenda Sue and me, and started working together getting the first cot ready to be slept in, it seemed a little strange to me, too. Especially as we were working at it half in the dark, with the only light being moonlight, filtering in onto the porch through some pines near the house, so that a sheet stretched out on a cot seemed to catch the only light there was, like a sponge. It was hard not to notice it, or not to find it somewhat strange to be working around in the moonlight, a boy and a girl who had just met, suddenly making up a bed. In fact, it must have seemed strange to Brenda Sue, too, because we ended up making up both the cots without either of us once mentioning the fact that this was what we were actually doing. Mostly we talked about the moonlight, and how somewhere out there on the creek was the lost skiff I was looking for, which, if only I was lucky enough, I might find tomorrow. Then the cots were ready, and Brenda Sue walked to a place where you could see the creek through the trees, and for a minute we looked at it, not saying anything, seeing it through the screen and the pines, but still clear and shining down below us, curving away out of sight. Then Brenda Sue said, "If you should not find it tomorrow, Rodney, will you look again for it later?"

I thought about it, and I knew I would. "It is a funny thing," I said, "but it already seems like I have been looking for that lost skiff forever. I don't guess I could ever give up on it altogether now. I would just have to keep looking."

We were quiet, watching the creek again. Then we heard Jack coming back toward the porch where we were, ready to go to bed now, I supposed. "If you don't find it tomorrow," Brenda Sue said, "I will keep on looking for it, too."

Then we said good night and she left, and I went in and thanked the Byrds again and said good night to them, and then Jack and I went to bed. I had meant to stay half awake, to see how Jack was making out through the night, but I guess I was tireder than I knew, because the last thing I remember was this kind of picture that came to my mind for a while, not exactly a dream, but not something clearly thought about, either, a picture in my mind of Brenda Sue in one boat and me in another, each of us rowing alone but out somewhere on the creek, looking for the same lost skiff.

12

Sometime in the night I seemed to hear a kind of moaning, and for a while I kept trying to shut out the sound of it; but then it came to me that it might be Jack, in pain, and I woke up with a jerk and looked around. But it was only a wind that had come up, blowing through the screen. Far off across the creek the moon was starting to go down, and in the last of the light I could see Jack stretched out on his back on his cot across from me, his left hand and wrist lying on his chest, kind of curved and big and strange-looking, as though it was hardly a part of him, like a sleeping cat. Yet I bent close and looked, and it was his bent hand and swollen wrist all right; and with the wind moaning in his ear and his wrist broken, Jack was sleeping.

For a minute, bending close and hearing the moaning sound of the wind and seeing Jack's easy breathing as he slept, with his hurt wrist lifting up and down on his chest as he breathed, it kind of gave me a chill, strange as that may sound, as though I had waked up in a different place than I had expected, and was suddenly not certain about who I was or who Jack was or even where we were, as though even time wasn't certain. It could have been some kind of cave I had waked up in, with only the sound of the wind to tell me where I was, and only moonlight to let me turn and see Jack, like a dumb, hurt animal, asleep in his pain. Then I lay back down and after a while it all straightened out for me, and I was sorry that I had thought of Jack that way; still, for a minute, that is how it had struck me. Then the moon went down and there was only the sound of the wind blowing through the porch screen, reminding me where I was; and I thought, well,

I guess we are all still animals at that, strange as it seems; and then I went back to sleep.

I woke up in the morning half certain that it would be raining, that the wind that had waked me in the night was due to a storm coming on, and that my chance would be gone to get down to the basin and find out if the skiff Mr. Byrd had seen was really the one I had lost. Yet when Jack shook my shoulder and I opened my eyes, it seemed that the wind was blowing gusts of sunlight everywhere I looked, with the porch screens shining with it, trembling in the wind, and the pine limbs dipping and bending so hard that even the pine needles had the glint of actual needles to them; I looked, and there was not a cloud anywhere in sight.

"This wind is no good," Jack said, "it will slow you down for sure. But at least it's out of the southwest, which will help keep water in the basin so that you can get in to the point all right. What worries me most is that somewheres behind it there is probably a storm."

"We have come through one storm already," I said, "although I have to admit that another one could be a nuisance. How is your wrist?"

"The same as since I broke it. Broke." I looked at him, and while his color was better than it had been the day before, there were some wrinkles between his eyebrows that had not been there before that gave him a kind of steady puzzled look, although more than anything else, he looked tired. "To tell you the truth, it has come to be a bother. I feel like a skittish bitch with six tits and eight pups; there just ain't no right way to be. This sling helps some, though."

"I had better hurry then," I said, "so I can get gone, and you can call your father." While I got dressed, Jack sat on the other cot and, talking low, told me that he had already talked to the Byrds about my going on down to the basin alone, and while they hadn't thought it was such a smart idea, they had agreed that he could hang around until I got back in the evening and took him with me back up the creek to The Landing. "To be honest," Jack said, "they thought it was crazy, especially when they made me let them see my wrist.

But I was stubborn and they give in." Then he laughed. "Ha," he said, "imagine the looks on their faces when as soon as you are well out of sight I tell them I have changed my mind completely. They will believe I have went crazy for sure. If I say so myself, the thing I am best noticed for is my stubbornness."

"I will leave right now," I said, "I won't even bother with breakfast." I could smell it cooking by this time, and it sure smelled good, but I figured the sooner I got away from the Byrds the sooner Jack's father could come for him.

"There's not that much of a hurry," Jack said, "and anyhow, you may need all the strength you can get before you have made it back to The Landing by yourself."

"I'll take that chance," I said. And Jack was still arguing about it when I went in to thank the Byrds and to say goodby, and they all argued with me, too, all except Brenda Sue, who just kept watching me, like she understood. So finally I lied and said I almost never ate any breakfast anyhow, and then I thanked them all once again, and went down to the pier, with Jack and Brenda Sue coming with me, Jack giving me directions all the while about how to find the point, the place where Mr. Byrd had seen the skiff. "You stay on the west bank, the way you have been doing, and along about midmorning you will find the creek is running almost due south, with most of the landings already left behind you, and just cypress swamp on either side. Then you just keep going straight until the next thing you see, straight ahead of you, will be Lucian's Fishing Camp, a kind of big old shack with about a hundred plywood skiffs tied up in front of it. It looks like the creek just stops there, but naturally it don't. It turns due west, and once you make that turn you are just about in the basin and practically at the point. You just keep going west, still keeping to the west bank, which actually will be to your north, and soon there will be nothing but marsh at your side, with the marsh grass thick and higher than your head. You keep watching it, to the north, and when you come to a break, the first one you come to, not much bigger than will let a boat through, you turn north there, and when you come out

128

on the other side of the marsh grass, ahead of you, about half a mile away, you will see the point. There are woods behind it, but the point itself sticks out into the marsh and has three big live oaks growing on it."

"Sounds simple enough," I said. I was anxious to get going. I had not done without breakfast just so I could sit around and listen to Jack tell me how to get down to the end of a creek. "I'll follow the creek to the basin, and in the basin I will look, to the north, for the point." And then I looked at Jack, who would know I was lying, and then to Brenda Sue, where I was telling the truth. "With luck," I said, "I will see you both this evening, pulling Mr. Haywood's cypress skiff behind me." Then I jumped down in the boat and started getting ready to leave.

But then Mr. Byrd came walking down the path from the house, and Brenda Sue said, "Wait," so I waited, watching Mr. Byrd taking his time and looking off down the creek as he came, until finally he got to the pier and came on out to the end.

"Rodney," he said, "the missis is worried that this wind will hold you back rowing, and I have this little three-horse motor you are welcome to use, and gas, if you think it will help you any. It would probably beat rowing, anyhow. You could take it back up to The Landing with you, you and Jack, and leave it with Mr. Matthews, and that way it would speed things up some in getting Jack to a doctor to see about that wrist of his."

I looked at Jack and he looked at me, and when I glanced at Brenda Sue she was looking down at the planks in the pier. We were tangled in our lie, and I believed she knew it. And for a minute I couldn't think of what to say, and Jack couldn't either, and then Brenda Sue said, "It's hardly a thing worth the offering, Pa."

He nodded. "It's not much," he said, agreeing with her, "but it might be of help."

I felt like the worst sort of phony, and even Jack had his head hung down when I looked at him. I knew it was up to me to get us out of the mess somehow. Nice as the Byrds had been to us both, I was not going to go ahead and use his motor just to save myself some rowing, knowing that the question of Jack's wrist would be taken care of sooner than he knew. "Mr. Byrd," I said, "I am sure it is a fine motor, but it would not be fair of me to use it. You may not believe this, but I am somehow the sort of person that just naturally has bad luck with things not my own. As last summer I burned down my uncle's barn by mistake, and this summer, already, I have lost Mr. Haywood's skiff, the first time I ever used it. I just could not take the risk with your motor. Thank you all the same, but it would be wrong if I did it. You can ask Jack; I am just no good with things I'm not used to, and I have never used an outboard motor in my life."

It was quite a little argument I had made, but it sounded truer than I had thought it would. I could see that Mr. Byrd was giving it some thought. "I hate to say it," Jack said, "but as long as Rodney has said it first, it is every word the truth. Through no fault of his own, in a case such as this, he is hardly to be trusted."

Seemed to me that this was going a little too far; made me sound like some kind of a nut. But I sat there, feeling the wind blow my hair around, all ready to go, smiling up at Mr. Byrd as though I had never heard of truer words being spoken. Finally Mr. Byrd shook his head. "Well," he said, "I would take the risk, but I would not have you feel beholden. I'll explain it to the missis as best I can." Then he shook his head again. "I most certainly hope you find that skiff," he said, and then he turned and started back up the path to his house.

Then there was just the three of us, quiet for a bit, and then Jack said, "If you find it or not, Rodney, no one can say you haven't tried." Then he surprised me. He turned to Brenda Sue, and like I might have been someplace else, he said, "You might not believe it, but Rodney there is a good old boy," and then without saying good-by to me or anything else, he turned and walked off the pier and on up toward the house.

Which left just Brenda Sue and me, neither of us knowing much what to say. "Well," I said, "I better get going, if I am going to find that skiff and get back here before dark," and I untied the rope and started drifting off.

"Rodney," Brenda Sue said, "there is no need for you to fight that wind too much. I will see you before dark, no matter what."

I was not at all sure what she meant by that, sounding so certain about it. I was still drifting, with the wind starting to blow me up the creek, the wrong way. "You will?" I said to her, shouting a little over the wind.

She nodded her head yes, and laughed, her hair blowing in the wind and the sound of her laughing being blown out to me. "Yes," she said, calling out so that I could hear her plain, her voice sounding happy and excited, it seemed, "I have got Pa's motor that you left me."

And then I started rowing and she stood there smiling and waving in the wind, until all I could see was the shape of her, a kind of darkness, standing there, growing smaller, shining in the sun and kind of shimmering in the wind, the way it is in the movies sometimes when what they mean to show you is something in a dream. Only I knew it was real.

I was surprised at how quick Byrd's landing faded away back down the river and was lost from sight, strong as the wind was at my back, and as slow as it seemed to me I was rowing. Then I was alone on the creek, with not another boat or a landing anywhere in sight, with the wind a kind of steady racket in my ears, and the water blown into a million little pointed waves, all sparkling in the sun, and with the boat going slow against the wind but kind of light and bouncing, even so. And for a while I didn't even think much about where it was I was going, or why. I just rowed, knowing I was alone, for sure, and with a long way to go, yet feeling a kind of excitement, just to be there rowing along alone in the wind, with the sunlight on the waves half blinding me, feeling strong and being satisfied with that, just glad to be alive, I guess, and not feeling worried or lonely at all. And I stayed surprised at how I moved right along, more than equal to the wind. For a while, now and then I would even discover I was

131

on the point of saying something out loud, some little thing I had noticed or thought about, like the strange stiffness of a dead cypress along the near shore, like a skeleton, with all around it the live green trees, bending in the wind, or even thinking strangely to myself about a thing my science teacher had said once, meaning nothing to me then, that high above the earth there are no winds, and thinking now, surprising myself at the thought, well, then, that is not the place where heaven is, and almost thinking it out loud, as though I was somehow not really alone at that. And while I have never thought about such things, I thought about it for a time, about being alone, and all the other things you see that may seem to be alone, too, but you have seen them, and so maybe in some way you are being seen as well. It sure seemed that way, at least. Or else why was I half the time about to talk out loud? Or if that seems crazy, then why didn't it feel crazy? Because it didn't. It hardly seemed a bad mistake.

I thought about it, and finally I thought, well, if a bird lets out a call, what does he really know about where it gets heard? And why should a man think he is so much different? So just for the hell of it, I stopped and coasted a bit and let the wind swing the boat around while I took a deep breath and let out a crazy, wild kind of yell, high up and loud, a kind of sound I could not remember ever having heard or made before. And I don't know why this should have pleased me, but it did, like I had finally hollered hello to the whole crazy world, or to whatever there was in it that might have heard me at least.

And then I went back to rowing, and, thinking about it, it didn't strike me as being altogether the most foolish thing I had done yet in my life, at that. To be honest, it half seemed to me that whatever it was I had hollered, it had been the first true thing I had ever said on my own.

Rowing along, it finally started fading in my mind, and I could see that it probably wasn't just something about being alone on the creek in the wind that had somehow got to me in this unusual way, but a more usual thing with me, too, which is to say, girls, or in this case a girl, in particular, Brenda Sue Byrd. Babe Honey Byrd. It would have made sense, it seemed to me, if I had let out a holler just about such a name alone. Plus the fact of the girl. But that was not the whole of it, either. It was the whole situation. And a wind, while it will always come to be an aggravation in time, sometimes, in a good strong wind, I will get caught by it, so to speak. There will be an excitement to it. It had happened before. Only this time, it hadn't caught me quite so much by surprise—barn burner, skiff loser, daydreaming girl watcher, all of it—it had caught me, for all of that, ready to look around at everything real, maybe not from as high as heaven or like Superman, but like a man in the wind, up high, anyhow, and looking around like a man at the world, more excited than afraid.

But then it pretty well faded, and I got back to thinking about the skiff I was looking for, and about Brenda Sue, and just what she might have meant about having her father's motor that I had left her and seeing me before dark, even though I had already said I would make it back to their landing by that time on my own. Whatever it was that she was so certain about was something I could only wonder on, and in time I pretty much gave up on it, as the wind, instead of helping ease the heat, seemed only to increase it, like a million gnats swarming around and being a nuisance, while I rowed along and the wind couldn't even manage to dry my sweat, but only hold me back and make me work that much harder.

Up ahead then, I saw some landings and houses coming into view, and I went back to thinking about Mr. Haywood's skiff that I was looking for, and I got hopeful about it again, believing that this time, alone, I might finally find it. I remembered the awful feeling that day when I had come back out of the woods and down to the creek and found the skiff gone, the way I could see it so clear in my mind, standing there looking around and not seeing it anywhere in sight; and now I saw it that clear again, smooth and clean-looking, plain bare wood, dark and solid, and perfect, except for the one small piece broken out of one end. The nicest little skiff I had ever seen. And I had been the one to lose it; and now, if anyone was going to find it, it was also going to be me. I was sorry—I really was—that Jack had been acting foolish and got his wrist broken, and I was glad he waited, much as it must have hurt him, and let me come looking for the skiff alone. But this was the way I had wanted it all along, and for once, the way it happened, even though it had been me that had given the boat the actual shove that broke Jack's wrist, I just couldn't keep telling myself that it was all my fault. It wasn't, and I knew it.

So I swung in closer to the shore, noticing that most of the landings were strung out ahead along the west bank, while way over on the east bank, as well as I could make out against the distance and the sun, there was nothing but a couple of houseboats tied up to the shore. Then I started coming up to the piers, and I slowed down and one by one looked over all the different kinds of boats that were tied up to the different piers, big ones and little ones, new and old, all different sizes and shapes and colors and all bobbing about in the wind and the waves and straining at their ropes like they were all half alive and wanted nothing so much as to break loose and drift off and get lost. But as many as they were and as different as they were, when I finally got on down a long straight stretch of creek and then halfway around a long slow bend and came at last to the end of the landings and piers and boats, I had not yet seen a single skiff that even looked like the one I had lost.

I guess I really hadn't expected to. For some reason, I finally was almost sure I would not ever find it tied to some ordinary pier, but in a place off by itself, about as far away as it could get from the place where I lost it, such as down at the end of the creek, at the point in the basin, where Mr. Byrd had seen it, or one just like it at least. It surprised me, but I couldn't say I was even disappointed. Having come this far down the creek, it just wouldn't have seemed right not to keep going on down to the end; and now I not only had the same old reason still to keep going, but it had more or less boiled down to being my last real chance as well. Find the skiff or not find it, win or lose, for this one time there was just this one last thing left for me to do, and I would know at least that I had actually done all that I could have done. It was a good feeling. It was what I had promised I would do.

Then far up ahead I noticed an empty clearing, just a green spot opening up between the trees along the bank, where the bank kind of jutted out, with not even a pier coming out from it, or a boat tied up to a tree or pulled up on the shore, and I made for it, remembering that I had not stopped to eat breakfast yet, with half the morning already gone. When I got there I saw that it was a bigger clearing than it had looked like from a distance, but just as bare and empty as I had thought it was, with no sign of use about it at all, not even any old beer cans thrown about, the way I had been noticing them now and then thrown up in the bushes and along the shore since I had left Byrd's landing. It seemed a good place to stop for a while, and I pulled the boat up a ways on the shore and tied it to a stump, the only one that was there, and got a can of pears and some crackers and a jar of Polish sausage and went to the back of the clearing, where there was a kind of a bank with some trees growing at the top of it that cut off some of the wind and gave some shade.

The food didn't taste at all like the smell of the breakfast Mrs. Byrd had been cooking when I had left, but it was food and I was used to it by this time, and I was hungry, so I ate and was done with it fairly quick. Then I just sat there for a time, resting, and looking around me and out at the river. I could see that the place where I was sitting was one of the highest bits of ground along the western bank, the highest since I had left the Byrds'; and I figured that at one time it had been even higher and had stuck out farther into the creek, because I could see how the creek had undercut the bank and spilled the top of it down into the water, making it only the third place of shallow water and a sandy bottom that I had come to on both the Little Star and the Big Star yet, with all the distance I had traveled. The way I was sitting, and the way the creek curved back the way I had come, it was like I was sitting somewhere out toward the middle of the creek, looking straight back up it, almost as if I was on some kind of

135

an island. It was about as nice a clearing, with as clear and long a view of the creek, as I had found. I was surprised that Jack had not told me about it, especially as it seemed to just be there, unused and belonging to no one, and a perfect place, for whatever reason, to stop for a while.

Far out in the creek I watched some mullet jumping, three or four of them, swimming up the creek and sort of taking turns at jumping, it seemed, shooting up out of the shining water and flashing in the wind, like mirrors to the waves below, and then dropping down again almost without a splash, or without changing the way of the waves at all. I watched them until they had gone so far up the creek they seemed hardly more than little flecks of light when they jumped. And then coming down the creek I saw the small dark shape of a boat, in near the west bank, a motorboat with only one person in it, with the boat so far away that I couldn't hear the motor yet, but could only see it bouncing easy in the waves and moving along, with somebody small sitting in the back that I guessed was a girl. Then I could hear the faint sound of the motor, fading and rising in the wind, and then getting steadier and louder, and I could see the girl's hair now and then whip about, a quick dark flash in the air, and somehow I knew it was Brenda Sue.

But I waited until she was close enough so that I was sure of it; and by that time she must have seen my boat, because she swung in closer toward the shore and I got up and stepped out into the sun and waved and ran down to the edge of the clearing and waited, seeing her wave back once, and then get closer, looking so small, somehow, in her father's big boat, with the river stretched out so wide and windy behind her, while she sat there, with only her hair moving, being tugged around by the wind. Then she was close and she turned and cut the motor and then turned back and just sat there watching me, letting the boat drift on in, not paying any attention to it, and not smiling, almost as though she was uncertain about my being glad to see her so soon again. Then I caught the bow of the boat and pulled it up on the shore and fussed around getting it grounded good. And when I looked up, she

136

was still sitting there on the back seat, and it gave me kind of a shock, the way she looked, so beautiful, her face so serious and her eyes so big, her hands folded in her lap, almost like a scared kid, it seemed. And then I noticed she was wearing tan-colored shorts and a blouse so much like the color of her skin that it startled me; and maybe I showed this somehow in my glance, because for a good while longer, even after I had said hello and something about how glad I was to see her again, she still just sat there, without having even smiled yet, as though it would make her half embarrassed just to stand up. I guess I must have stared.

"Pa sent me to bring a message to you," was the first thing she said.

I was still standing there holding onto the boat, like it might float away if I moved. "About Jack?" I said.

She nodded. "His father has come and got him, and you are to be back at their landing no later than Saturday noon, with the skiff if you have found it, but without it if it still should be lost. That's all of it. Pa thought you should know."

"To tell the truth," I said, "I have known it all along. But I sure am glad you have gone to this trouble to come and tell me."

"I have known it all along, too," she said.

"I had guessed as much," I said.

"I figured you had," she said.

Then for a minute I couldn't think of what to say next, and I guess Brenda Sue couldn't either, and we just stayed there, looking at each other, with the sun beating down on us and the wind blowing our hair around, not either one of us even smiling, and then I said, "Well, I am sorry to have put you to so much trouble for nothing, but if you are not in a big hurry to get back up the creek, there is not much sense in our staying out here in this wind and hot sun like we are. Back up by that bank there is some shade."

Just for a second then, Brenda Sue smiled, or started to, and then in that straight honest way I had noticed before, she said, "Rodney, if I had not wanted to see you again, I would have told Pa the truth and stayed at home to start with. You are

137

right, it is hot here in the sun." Then she stood up and walked toward me as easy as if she was walking along a path, stepping up on the seats when she came to them and jumping down as light as a cat, and when she got to the end of the boat I held out my hand, not to help her, and she took it, not needing any help, and I held onto it and she held on, and we walked back up across the clearing to the shade.

13

I don't know how long it was that Brenda Sue and I stayed there at that clearing, but I believe it was longer than either of us had meant it to be. Because first it was strange, being altogether alone, just the two of us, back up under the bank in the shade, where no one could see us or even hear us talk, with no one to look at but each other, and yet with no place else to look, either, except out at the creek, with the sun so bright on the water that you could hardly stand it, and with it seeming like we were practically on an island, sitting there side by side so close that when we looked at each other it was almost like we had touched. It took us some time just to get used to it, and it was somehow not always the easiest thing in the world to find something natural to talk about. Particularly after we had used up the subjects of Jack's broken wrist and the lost skiff and the unusualness of the weather. After that, there seemed nothing left to talk about but us, which we hardly needed called to our attention.

Yet we got used to it finally. And more than that, if I am going to stay honest about it. Without all the details, there was some time passed in this way, too. Considerable.

But unless I should seem to be hinting at some bigger deal than there actually was, maybe I should stop right here and make it clear that nothing was done that would shame either Brenda Sue or me if it were to be known, or which we should have to worry about in the days to come, if that is plain enough.

Maybe this should not really have had to be said, but without the details, some doubts might be left, and there can be details in things between a boy and girl, it seems to me, wonderful in themselves, but somehow dead wrong in the telling.

And which won't be told by me, anyhow. In the name of honesty, I will only say that there is a limit to the way a boy and girl can get to know each other just by talking, especially if what they have got around to talking about is how surprising it is the way it seems they have known each other forever. In a case such as that, I found out then even two of the shyest people in the world can come to the limit of their words. And then they'll just naturally find some other ways of finding out and knowing more, not just how they feel about each other, but how they actually feel. Which I have said less nicely than it happened. But while this is a general subject surely better known by others than by me, and no big news to the world, still it seems to me that the details are no more the same for everyone than are people's fingerprints. And this kind of specialness, these details, because we're born that way, I guess, no two alike, is no one's business but my own. In this case, mine and Brenda Sue's. And that is every bit as honest as I mean to get.

Except to say that for a time, at least, I have never been less clumsy in my life.

And then somehow time had slipped well on into the afternoon, surprising us both, and while I didn't say anything about it, it began to seem to me that it didn't look as though I would be able to get down to the basin and back up to Byrd's landing before dark after all. But it had been so unexpected and perfect a day up until then that I couldn't let it worry me too much. Even so, I might have still had time enough if I hadn't decided that it would not be right to let Brenda Sue start back for the landing, a thing we had finally started talking about, at least, without having some food first, something we both had forgot all about. For a while she argued that she shouldn't take any more of my time, that I was a good ways off from the basin still and that finding Mr. Haywood's skiff was more important. But then I convinced her that we could at least have a kind of dessert together, if not a regular meal such as Jack and I had been used to, and I went down to the boat and got out the can of pitted yellow cherries I had been cooling in the fish well, and the tin of homemade cookies Mrs.

140

Haywood had sent along, and we took the time to eat the can of cherries and some cookies together. And then I still might have had time to make it there and back by dark, if I rowed hard enough, if it hadn't been for one last thing. We had finished eating and were standing up and looking around, getting used to the idea, it seemed, of going two separate ways again, which was strange, how strange this could have come to seem to us in so short a time. And then Brenda Sue looked off up the river and shook her head. "It's hard to believe," she said, "that two days ago we did not even know that each other was alive. And yet here we are. When you first saw me coming, did you know it was me?"

"I hoped it was," I said, and then I said, "I will never forget it."

"I will tell you something, Rodney," she said. "Coming down the creek with Pa's message for you, I kept thinking that I had a kind of message for you, too, only I was sure I would be too scared to come out and say it, that you might misunderstand or just not care. And I was still not sure if I should tell you or not, when I caught up with you here. Because I could see what a hurry you must be in to find that skiff, to have got this far so quick. And anyhow, this didn't seem the place to talk about anything. I guess you don't know it, but hardly nobody comes here any more. Not since several years ago, when they found the dead nigger here, floated ashore. That's what it's called now, Dead Nigger Point. Yet even so, I won't forget it, either. Our being here."

"Dead Nigger Point?" I said.

"How could you have known?" Brenda Sue said.

It was foolish what I said then, as though I still hadn't heard her right. "Is that all it's ever called? Not just Dead Man's Point or something?"

"I don't know," Brenda Sue said, looking at me sort of surprised. "If it had of been a white man, I guess that's what they would have called it, Dead Man's Point, or something like that. But it was a nigger." I guess what surprised me most of all was the easy way she said it, like she didn't even notice it, the word nigger. "Didn't Jack ever mention it to you?"

141

"No," I said.

"It was an awful thing," she said. "They say he might have been killed and not just drowned. There were all sorts of stories. And they never even found out who he was. Hardly more than a child, Pa said. But that was years ago, Rodney. I was hardly more than a child myself. I'm surprised that Jack had not told you about it before."

And for a second or two all I wanted to do was to forget it, as though it was just something that had come up by accident and had nothing to do with Brenda Sue and me at all. I could see Brenda Sue watching me, sort of puzzled but smiling a little, and I thought that what she was probably waiting for was only for me to ask her what it was that she had been about to say, her own message that she wasn't scared to tell me now. And then a feeling came over me worse than when I had seen my uncle's barn going up in flames, or when I had come down to the edge of the creek and found Mr. Haywood's skiff gone, a sick feeling, that everything had changed so fast and gone wrong, somehow because of me, and with no way left for me alone to make it right. I never wanted harder just to forget a thing in all my life. Because if I didn't, then whatever I said would not be at all what Brenda Sue was expecting, and after all we had said and done, it could hardly seem fair or right to her. And I knew it was true. It wouldn't be fair or right, because with the time we had spent together, and knowing Alabama as well as I did, I had never bothered to take the time or to take the chance to let her know, as I had done with Jack, how I felt about some things. And the way she stood there, just smiling and waiting and not knowing, it half killed me, knowing that whatever I said I would probably say it wrong and end up only hurting Brenda Sue's feelings and not helping some poor, dead, unknown black man at all, or anyone else, black or white, and certainly not myself. And the thing that struck me as most crazy, the saddest thing of all, was standing there realizing almost for the first time that Brenda Sue was so darkly colored herself, and that from the first I had liked her for it, her own special color, the way she was so beautiful and so special in every other way, too.

And then I said it about as wrong as it could be said. "Speaking only for myself," I said, practically like I was talking to a stranger, "if a man is dead and unknown and possibly murdered, that seems enough. I could not see a reason for calling him nigger as well."

It was like I had slapped her in the face. She pulled back, her smile still lasting for a second or two, and the waiting look still sort of showing in her face and eyes. I had caught her that much by surprise, so that even as she pulled away, like I had hit her, she was still smiling and waiting, still not expecting trouble at all, even though it had already come. Then her face went blank. If she had turned her back to me, or held her hands up over her face, her expression could not have been more hidden, that quickly, from my sight. She just looked at me, as though I had gone that blank to her, too. I had said it too sudden, too stupid, and all wrong. And I stood there staring at her and not knowing what else to say. I felt like a freak.

And then finally I said, "I am sorry, Brenda Sue. I didn't mean to sound so smart like that. I guess I was mostly surprised. I mean I know this is Alabama and people will say nigger without thinking much about it, while back home when they say it they will always mean something ugly; but even so, somehow it surprised me, to hear you say the word so easy. Especially you."

The way she stepped back a step and stiffened up, I knew, almost for certain—suddenly understanding what it must always have been like for her, growing up so dark-colored in a place where this could be something so serious that you wouldn't even be teased about it to your face, where no one would dare, but where you would still always wonder what was being whispered about it behind your back—I knew I had said the wrong thing again, for sure, saying how the word had surprised me, especially from her, the word nigger.

Then she took a quick little breath, and for just a second she tried to smile, as though she was trying to remind me how friendly we had been, still able to smile, even with something as awful as this that had already happened, so that we could somehow work it out and stay friends, if I just didn't make it impossible, if I would just have enough sense not to come right out and mention her own dark color. "I would just like to know," Brenda Sue said, "what you meant by me especially?"

I had guessed right. There was no doubt of it left in my mind. Well, I thought, now you have done it, for sure; because if you try and stand here and lie about something real like this, you won't fool her for one second, and she will think that all you are interested in is the fact that she is a girl. And if you go ahead and lie, that will be the truth, you will be doing it for just that reason. She is not going to kill you or hurt you or even be hurt herself if you tell the truth; but she is apt to tell you to go to hell and mean it. Although at first, it may hurt her feelings some, at that, if you say it wrong, which you probably will.

I don't know how long I stood there thinking to myself about it; not long, I guess, but it seemed long. But I finally just went ahead and took a chance, a chance with both of us, that her feelings might get hurt, no matter how I said it, and that I might get told to go back where I had come from and the sooner the better. "I'll tell you what I meant by that, " I said. "It would not have surprised me, for instance, if it had of been Jack, even though his mother is against saying nigger, and we have argued it out a few times ourselves. But you have to admit that there is nothing either shy or what you might call sweet about Jack. He is apt to say about anything that comes to mind, with one word as good as another, just so long as you know what he is talking about. I would not say that any of this seems true of you. The truth is, I have never met a nicer person than you in my life, nicer acting, or more nicely shy and sweet and everything. Or nicer-looking. That is what I mean by you especially, surprising me, saying nigger so easy. I did not mean the fact that you are far more dark-colored than some girls, but I'm not afraid to say I noticed it, either, if this is what you think I meant. Naturally I have noticed it. I have just never bothered to wonder about it. To me, all it is is beautiful. I hope I have not put it wrong."

144

"Well," Brenda Sue said, "I do not like hints is all."

"I am too stupid for hints," I said. "If I say something wrong, I generally just say it. Have you noticed any hints?"

"No," she said. "You have put it pretty plain, I guess. You don't like your friends saying nigger."

I thought about it a second, and then I said, "Well, I believe I said some other things, too."

Then Brenda Sue seemed to relax a little, like the worst was over, even though I had mentioned the fact of her dark-colored skin clear enough. "Ma's folks have both some Greek and French about them," she said. "I reckon that's where the color comes from. It is hardly something we talk about. But I guess it's something you would have to notice. I have noticed it all right. Mostly I have noticed how other people notice, without ever saying."

"Well," I said, relaxing again a little myself, "I have said it, and I hope I haven't said it wrong."

"You said it nice," she said. Then she stopped, as though she wasn't sure about what she was going to say next, and then she said it anyhow, trusting me, I guess. "I have thought about it a lot; and I used to be bothered, you know, and then I would think how awful it must be, well, to be really colored."

"It hardly seems fair," I said.

Then I could see the real trouble was over, and we both stopped standing around so stiff and uncertain about everything and started smiling and talking about this and that again, and it was all pretty much the way it had been before, except that it took an hour, probably, just standing around, and then getting both the boats back in the water and starting to say good-by, but holding off, only now and then coming back to the thing that had caused the trouble in the first place, a little thing, I guess, and hardly worth the trouble it had caused us, but getting to where we could talk about it like it was something we had known about between us forever, even though we never really got quite natural about it at that, not altogether, like there was something important about it, even so, the word nigger. Something wrong.

And it wasn't until Brenda Sue and I had finally said good-by, and she had gone on up the creek and I had started on down it again, with some signs of evening already in the air and the wind blowing just as hard if not harder than it had been blowing all day, that I thought about it, and realized that it must have been really important, after all; or else how could it have come so close to ruining everything between us?

And what Brenda Sue had meant to tell me, and what she had finally told me, and the reason we hadn't had to hurry too much, although in the end we had spent a good hour or so longer there on the clearing than we had meant to, was the message that tomorrow her mother would be gone all day with her father, visiting kin in Mobile. That was all. She would be home, all day, alone.

It was the last thing she told me before she started back up the creek, and it was about the straightest thing she had told me yet. There were a million ways she could have said it, I guess, pretending it was something she had just remembered or had just happened to think about, or somehow saying it as though it didn't mean a thing, and going on by it and leaving me to figure it out for myself. But she didn't do it that way at all. She just said it, and then stood there looking at me, serious and scared. And I knew that by then she wasn't afraid that it might not matter to me, but only that I might misunderstand.

"To tell the truth," I said, "the big reason I started out in such a hurry to get down to the basin this morning wasn't so much to find out if Mr. Haywood's skiff was there, but so I could get back and have a chance to see you one last time. Just to see you. But here I have already seen you today, and late as it is, I will have to camp for the night at the point; so I will stop and see you tomorrow, too. I'll have to get started back up to Mr. Haywood's landing, of course, so I won't stay long. But it sure will be nice to see you again."

Seeing how serious she had been about it, and how scared, it seemed, it had made me talk kind of fast and foolish, as though I didn't want to admit what I knew was on our minds. Being alone, I mean. It was like it actually scared me, too.

146

And looking at her, I knew I hadn't got honest the way she had or leveled with Brenda Sue one bit, and I knew she knew it. So I tried again. "Brenda Sue," I said, "I'm glad you weren't afraid to tell me, because otherwise I would have rowed my head off trying to get down to the basin and back up to your landing to see you tonight. And then I would have started back up the creek by moonlight, and tomorrow would have been lost. But if you are worried at all, I will tell you something. I am the sort of person who can make all kinds of mistakes and say the wrong things and even burn a barn by accident or lose a skiff through ignorance, and I am far from perfect when it comes to the things I may happen to notice or to think, and I won't pretend a thing different. But when it comes to people, I believe I can be trusted."

It was wonderful to watch and see the worry leave her face. Then we said good-by, and soon Brenda Sue was out of sight going back up the creek and I was alone again, rowing hard against the wind, with the sun getting low in the sky off to my left, while I rowed down the last, long, straight stretch of Big Star Creek, due south, with far ahead, just coming into view, Lucian's Fishing Camp, with one last chance still left to me before dark of finding the skiff, a skiff—with all that had happened that seemed to have nothing to do with it or even with my looking for it—that was still a real skiff, and still was lost.

For a while it was good just to go along rowing my crazy head off and thinking about nothing else, or trying to anyhow, except such a simple thing as a skiff I had lost and was trying to find. It seemed to me, when it crossed my mind now and then, that back there at the point some things had got pretty complicated for a while. Well, I thought, I guess nothing is really simple at that, not even a thing like starting out down a creek with nothing else in mind but trying to find a skiff that had drifted off and disappeared. But then I just rowed, and rowed hard, and kept it as simple again as I could.

Then I guessed I must be getting near to the basin and the bay, because the fishing camp was just up ahead and I could

147

smell a different smell blowing in off the water. And then a sea gull, the first I had seen, came sailing in from the west, blown in by the wind, and right over my head he tilted sideways and slipped on down and kind of hung there, gliding on the wind, looking at me, so close I could see his eyes, as though he was wondering as much about where I had come from and what I was doing there as I was wondering about him. Then he gave a push with his wings and sailed up and off ahead of me toward the fishing camp, and I thought, well, as far as a sea gull is concerned, all I am doing out here in this wind at the end of Big Star Creek is looking for a skiff I lost, although there is more to this than would meet his eye, high as he flies and carefully as he looks. On the other hand, I thought, there is a chance he has seen Mr. Haywood's skiff and even knows right now where it is, so why should I feel so smart about it, just because I'm a man, while a sea gull is only a bird. Then he came sailing back, high overhead, not even interested enough any more to drop down for a second look, and then he flew back off the way he had come, showing me how easy a thing like that could be done, while I just sat there, rowing, but feeling again, even so, a kind of excitement, the way it had been when I started out in the morning and had somehow felt like some crazy kind of a bird myself, caught up in the wind. And then I rowed on past the fishing camp, still feeling that way, feeling strong and happy and not really caring if things were simple or complicated or both at once, and not worried about anything, not even bothered any more by the wind, as though a curious sea gull, of all things, had showed me again the way things really were. Or the way they could be, anyhow.

14

With the directions Jack had given me, finding my way out into the basin and through the opening in the marsh grass was so simple that it seemed I must have done it sometime once before. Anyhow, when I rowed through the opening and came out into the shallow water on the other side and turned around and looked, the first thing I saw was the point, off in the distance, with the three big live oaks right at the end of it, their leaves blowing and shining in the sun, like a kind of natural beacon. I knew I had finally made it.

For a while I let the boat drift, seeing the shallow water spread out around me like the water in some giant pond, not blown into waves but only being rippled by the wind. It was the marsh grass, stretching away as far as I could see all around it, that caught the wind and made a sight I had never seen before, the tall thick grass bending and lifting in long sweeping dips and waves, as though whatever it was that it was fastened to, the ground it was growing on, was something that floated as well, the whole thing moving like one single floating thing. I knew it was only my surprise, but at first, sitting there in the boat, hardly drifting in the quiet water and seeing the marsh grass sort of rocking and waving in the sun, I had a feeling I was seeing something as unusual as if I had actually caught a glimpse of the whole round earth kind of rocking and spinning along in space. It was a feeling that surprised me, as if I really believed that the marsh and the shallow pond where I floated at the time, all of it and myself included, was a kind of miracle, which, with one big wind blowing hard enough, could be lifted loose from whatever held us in place, as easy as the ending of a dream. It was a sight I had never seen before anyhow, and a feeling I can hardly describe. I guess it should have puzzled me, as nature seldom gives me much of a feeling one way or another, or at least nothing to wonder about. And in this case I might have wondered what the hell was going on with my brains, and even worried about it, but actually it didn't bother me at all. To tell the truth, it seemed interesting, although I'm sure I cannot explain that, even to myself.

I drifted awhile longer and watched the marsh grass waving in the wind, and then I picked up the oars and started rowing toward the point, noticing how thick the shrimp grass was in the shallow water, looking down at it on either side of the boat and seeing how still and dark it looked in contrast to the wind in the marsh grass in the light of the evening sun, as though I was looking down at the top of some watery kind of forest where already it was night. And almost to the point, rowing along, wondering about this and about all the other things that had happened and had been new and different and in one way or another had surprised me since I started out with Jack with the simple purpose of looking for a skiff I had lost, it came to me as a kind of shock suddenly to realize that I was alone in a strange place and about to spend the night there and that it didn't worry me a bit. And this surprised me so much that I stopped rowing again for a minute, for no reason at all, and just sat there looking back the way I had come, as though there was something that had happened along the way that I hadn't noticed at the time, something I had missed, like I might have also missed the lost skiff, watchful as I had tried to be. Because back then, to start with, I could have done it, I knew, alone all the way; but it would have been something. And now, it didn't even seem strange.

And then as though I was certain I would find the skiff at the point, I started rowing again, rowing hard, like I was trying to make up for all the time I had lost, in all the ways that I had, since I first started, as though this could be done in the last few hundred yards. I was headed straight due north toward the three live oaks, but as I got close I could see that there was no good place to land there, and I swung to the west and out around a little strip of marsh grass. And then back to the east I saw the clearing under the three trees, a big one, flooded with sunlight coming in under the branches from behind me, with a wide, green stretch of crab grass coming down to the water's edge, and all of it, the big clearing and the wide, green grassy beach, empty. All I could see was the dark rounded pile of ashes left from a campfire back under the oaks, in the center of everything, like a cold hard rock that could have been there forever. I had come too late.

I rowed on in to the shore.

When I had pulled the front of the boat up onto the grass, I didn't do much for a time except wander stupidly around the clearing, looking about under the three big oaks and at the woods behind them, and then out at the marsh grass, waving in the wind, hearing the oak leaves making a soft singing sound as the wind blew through them, high up over my head, even looking up into the leaves, surprised at the thickness of them. I guess I was just trying to see where I was, and to get it through my head that I had made it down to the end of the creek and had gone as far as I could go. And the skiff was still lost.

The whole thing seemed strangely hard to believe, but finally I knew it was the simple truth, and I stopped wandering around looking at things and acting like some idiot walking in his sleep. I went down to the boat and got the ax. I will not, I thought, eat cold Polish sausage for one more meal; and whether I have failed to find the skiff or not, I still am hungry and I have got a right to eat.

I built a fire in the ashes that the other people had left there, and opened two cans of beef stew and heated it, and ate all of it, except what I'd burned on the bottom of the pot. By the time I had finished with that and with cleaning up my mess, the sense of strangeness that had bothered me was altogether gone. I looked around the clearing again, seeing it for what it was, not the empty end of a crazy searching trip, but a clearing, and a fine one at that. A nice place to spend the night.

I went down to the boat and got the tarp and brought it back up by the fire and folded it several times to make a kind of mattress, and then I brought up a couple of blankets and folded one for a pillow, and spread the other over the tarp. There was really no need of a fire, but I threw some more wood on it anyhow, and sat down beside it on the blanket and looked out at the water and the marsh grass, with the sun low in the sky and lighting up the waving tops of the marsh grass so that great glowing streaks of light seemed to go streaking and bending across the whole marsh, while the water down in front of me rippled and sparkled like a bright, steady starlight kind of fire, looking almost cool, warm as the evening was.

Okay, I thought, let the night come.

And all I did for the next hour or two—sometimes it seemed that time had stopped altogether, while other times it would seem to go shooting past me, so it is hard to be exact—was to sit there and think and watch the day blow away, so to speak, and night to come trailing in behind it, like its dust. I guess that is a thing I would not generally think of saying, but at the end, right as the sun was just half in sight at the farthest edge of the marsh, the whole sky turned into a thick, hanging sort of red-colored cloud, and it made me think of the clouds of dust I have seen in the evenings following cars up the dusty road past The Hill. And I believe there is some dust of sorts in all sunsets anyhow. But this one, with the wind blowing and the marsh spread out as far as I could see and the sun almost straight out in front of me, was about as great a sunset as I could ever hope for.

To tell the truth, it was terrific. There were times when I didn't have better sense than to stare right into the sun itself, as though with everything else the way it was, I might as well go blazing down myself. And while I would not recommend it as being good for the eyes, particularly somewhat weak eyes like my own, those few good stares I gave the sun are something, along with the marsh in the wind that evening, that I will most likely not forget.

I doubt if I will live out my life or even manage to die in some great blaze of glory, but at least I believe I have a hint now of what a word like glory means. It's in the world, at least. Whatever harm it may have done my eyes, I saw it.

Or else I don't know what it was I saw or felt, but it was something. And the surprising thing is that I am the sort that generally can take a sunset or leave it alone. But it probably was not just the sunset, either. In fact, I'm certain it wasn't. Because I didn't just sit there looking at the view, getting blinded by the sun and letting the wind blow through my empty brains. Or if the wind did sometimes sort of seem to be shoving my thoughts around, the thoughts were there anyhow, thick as marsh grass, just steady waves of them running through my head, like a dam in my memory had burst at the same time my eyes had been opened up, and I was remembering old things and thinking new ones practically together.

I won't try and say all the things I remembered and thought about, while another part of my mind was just sitting there watching the sun go down. But if I have made it seem like nothing but a great deal of confusion, the fault is mine. In the end, at least, when the sun was gone and the stars were out and the moon was lighting up the darkness of the woods behind me, it all seemed clear to me. With all the things I had remembered, chief of which, naturally, was my mother, and all the new things I had thought about, chief of which, also naturally, I suppose, was Brenda Sue, the one big single simple thing I had been remembering and seeing and thinking about the whole time was—what it had to be, I guess—life itself. And what had come to seem most clear to me about it was the endless wonder of it, even in a world where life itself ends, in a world where people die, in a world that will someday die itself. Even so, the biggest thing, the greatest thing of all is life. Unless, of course, there is actually a God, at that.

Which, as I lay wrapped in my blanket listening to the wind and the marsh's night sounds, watching the last few red coals of my fire glow bright in the wind and grow smaller and smaller, I decided that there was. That there is a God, I mean. I guess I didn't have to decide anything, really, but I decided it anyhow. I couldn't see any reason not to.

And I suppose it is an awful thing to admit, but later, just before I went to sleep, being thankful for the coolness of the wind and the fact that it kept the insects so well blown away, and thinking in a careless sort of way about the things that had happened on the trip down the creek and about Brenda Sue and tomorrow and the days to come, the thought went through my mind as clear as though I had said the words, I sure am glad Jack broke his wrist. It was the first real thought I had given to Jack in hours. It hardly seemed fair to him.

Then, hoping it wouldn't rain, I went to sleep.

Sometime during the night, unknown to me, the wind went down, and what woke me up, with the light just starting to show around the tops of the trees, was not the sun or birds singing but what must have been a dozen or so big swamp mosquitoes buzzing around my head and having a regular feast off my face and hands. This, and one big single drop of something wet that splashed down exactly on my ear, like it had been aimed. So I woke up startled and swatting at mosquitoes and looking around in the greyness, wondering what wet thing it was that had plopped down in my ear and where had it come from? I sat up, and worked at the mosquitoes for a time and then I got quiet and noticed the dampness and the wet smell in the air and a kind of dripping sound, like water left dripping from a faucet, high up in the leaves above my head. I listened, and felt a drop go plop on my hand, and I knew that even if it was so light a rain that I couldn't hear it or really feel it yet, up in the oak leaves it was raining, and that that was what I heard dripping down through the leaves and what had plopped into my ear as I slept. Rain.

I got up and walked out from under the trees and stood looking out at the marsh, seeing it as only a big, misty-grey flatness, not able to see the rain, but feeling it, anyhow, on my face and hands, like a soft, cool wind, a drizzle so light that instead of falling down, it just seemed to hang where it was. But it was rain all right.

In the dim, misty light, Mr. Haywood's white boat down at the water's edge was the brightest thing I could see, and even so it looked strange, small and blurred and like it might have been half floating in the mist itself. I went down to it, and it was still well up on dry ground and safe enough, but everything in it, the oars and the seats and the supplies that were in the open, was covered with water so thick that I could brush it off with my hand, as though the rain was so light that it was practically sticky and would just stay where it hit, without the weight to roll off. I grabbed a rag from under the front seat and tried to dry a few things, but it was like trying to clean up spilled paint, and I soon gave up on it and went back up and got my blankets and the tarp and came back and stored the blankets up in front and then spread out the tarp and fastened it the way Jack and I had done before. Which would keep things from getting any wetter, I figured, and would be ready to make into a tent again if worse came to worse later in the day and the drizzle decided to change itself into a pouring rain.

I went back up under the oaks and built a fire with some of the wood I had brought up the evening before. It wasn't light enough yet to leave for Byrd's landing, so I got a can of plums and the last can of hash and had breakfast while I waited, listening to the steady drip and plop of the rain in the leaves up over my head, but staying dry enough by the fire, noticing how the flames went straight up into the air, as calm and steady as the flame on a candle in a closed room. With a day this still, I thought, this rain will probably just hang around forever, because it sure won't be blown away, and at the rate it's falling it's hardly apt to rain itself out. And then I thought, well, how about that; less than a week out on a creek and I am an expert on the weather. So then I glanced back to the east, half expecting to see the sun come breaking through, but the sky, though lighter, was a solid dark grey and looked as though it meant to stay that way.

I waited until the marsh was in view as far as I could see and until I figured it was as light as the morning was going to get, letting the fire die down as I waited, and then I left, leaving the clearing the same as I had found it, except for some new ashes added to the old and a small streak of smoke from the last of the coals lifting up straight and lonely-looking into the air below the dripping oaks. Then I rowed out and headed south and with a few good strokes the clearing was out of view, and I let the boat coast, seeing how flat and still the water was, with the drizzle drifting down into it so slow and fine that it hardly showed as anything more than a kind of sheen, brightening the water, strangely, under so dark a sky. The marsh grass stood straight and still as a wall all around, and in the quiet I could only remember the evening before with the wind blowing and the water sparkling and the marsh grass bending and waving, and wonder, as I started rowing on again, how I could have stayed there at the point for just a matter of hours, less even than a day, and have it seem, as I rowed away from it, that I was leaving a place as well known to me as some place where I had spent months or even years.

Then I came to the opening in the marsh grass, and looking back, the three big oaks that marked the point were just one big misty cloud of green, looming up out of nowhere, it seemed, as though what was marked there was not so much a place as a mystery. I stopped and took one last look, and then, like some kind of an idiot, I actually gave it all a wave. Sitting there in a drizzle with my clothes already gone limp from it, water dripping down off my face and hands and down the back of my neck, with no living thing in sight anywhere around, I took one last look at the oaks and then lifted my hand and waved. It was about as crazy a thing as I have ever done, waving good-by to some trees and a place. But I did it. I sure was glad I was alone. Then I rowed on through the opening and out into the basin and headed back east, not worrying about the lost skiff or the rain or anything else, but thinking of Brenda Sue, and rowing hard, so used to rowing finally that it had come to seem like nothing at all.

15

Except for slowing when I went past Lucian's Fishing Camp to check if the skiff might possibly be in among all their plywood boats, and again when I went past a couple of houseboats and some landings, I never eased off my pace.

Neither did the drizzling rain.

I kept to the east bank, the way I had planned, but I didn't really expect to find Mr. Haywood's lost skiff among the few places scattered along there, and I didn't find it. However, I did try to keep it in mind, although that wasn't the easiest thing in the world to do. Seemed that the closer I got to Byrd's landing, the more my mind just seemed to go blank, and I would row along as though all I could think about was rowing. Toward the end, I would say that maybe some others had rowed this boat of Mr. Haywood's faster and farther, but none with better concentration or more like a machine. It was almost as though I had completely forgotten where it was I was going.

I hadn't, of course. Not at all.

I knew, all right. But for some reason or other it just seemed better not to think about it.

Although that is not quite the truth, either; I mean that "for some reason or other" business. I am not that dumb, even when I try to believe it myself. The reason I didn't want to think about it was that I knew that where I was headed was to see Brenda Sue and to see her alone, and on a rainy day at that, even if neither of us had planned on the rain. And I had never had a situation quite like that to think about before. In fact, nothing like that at all before, ever. Not going to see a girl alone who just naturally seemed to like me the way Brenda Sue seemed to like me, and with the crazy business of my being so scared around girls having somehow cut out altogether for me, and not to be counted on for any help.

And whatever this may show about me, I knew that thinking about all this wouldn't be much of a help, either. Far from it. So I just rowed, not even minding the rain. It was cool, at least. And if my mind wished to stay blank, I figured it probably knew best.

Anyhow, that was the way it happened. Then finally I came rowing around a bend and turned and looked over my shoulder up the creek ahead of me, and there it was on the other shore, the house up on the hill, looking small and dark in the distance. Down below it was the pier, just as I had remembered, sticking out into the creek, with the little tin roof out at the end shining in the rain, a landmark I couldn't miss, like a sign just for me, saying BRENDA SUE. I had reached Byrd's landing.

Then the rain seemed to blur my eyes and I could feel rain trickling down my neck, and for some reason the oar handles felt cold and clumsy in my hands. My breath wouldn't work right, and the thought went through my mind, I am too wet and dirty and I probably smell like a campfire or a wet dog, or both, and I have got no business barging in on Brenda Sue all alone like this, the way I am. And then I turned and headed across the creek for the landing and Brenda Sue.

I was glad she wasn't waiting out at the end of the pier, to watch me come rowing up in the rain and bang into it and then stumble around in the water in the back of the boat and then slip on the wet planks getting out on the pier, like I hardly knew how to dock a boat or get out of one. Once the boat was tied and I was safe on my feet and had straightened out my clothes as best I could, I felt considerably more like myself. Standing up, I am tall, at least, and I always stand straight. Even soaking wet.

Well, I thought, I'm a mess for sure, but maybe Brenda Sue won't mind too much; whatever it is that she happens to see in me, it is hardly apt to be the snappy way I dress. Then I started walking up the long curving path to the house, notic-

158

ing the silence and the emptiness all around, looking up once at the house and seeing how closed and empty it looked and wondering, with a kind of quick numb feeling in my stomach, if maybe the house was really empty and Brenda Sue was gone. I had hardly looked back down when I heard the first human sound I had heard since I landed. It went through me like a shock, although all it was was the simple slam of a screen door swinging shut.

The sound was still hanging in the air when I looked up and saw Brenda Sue standing on the steps looking down at me, and then she walked down the steps and started running down to meet me. Like a nut, I stopped and just stood there, watching her. I didn't even wave. What other girl in the world, I thought, wouldn't care, but would just come running? And I watched her, seeing the light-blue dress she was wearing blow back against her and lift up when she ran, suddenly knowing that she must have run like that down this same path a million times, since she was a kid, running just to be running; and now she was not just a kid, and was running to me. And however crazy it may sound, the way I saw her then, the way I felt, I knew there could never be a sight more wonderful to see, as though I saw her running down to me this way, from a little kid until finally now, down through all her life. For an instant, as though time held still, it was like that, I saw it all like that; and I just stood there, knowing that this was what I hadn't known before, ever, the real wonder of it, that it is not just two people, and not just now, but two whole lives. And then I didn't think she would really do it, but she hardly slowed, and we met, out in the open for anyone to see that was there to see, and I just picked her up and held her. And of all the dreams and thoughts I had ever dared to have about how some girl might really someday seem and feel to me, I had never dreamed or thought that a girl could surprise me so, and feel and seem, most of all, so precious. Just hanging on to me, being held by me in the rain; without even so much as a kiss having happened.

"I didn't find the skiff," I said.

"I know," she said. "I'm sorry."

Then I put her down. "I'm soaking," I said, "and must smell like a dog. I hope I have not got you all wet."

"It's all right," Brenda Sue said. "I should not have been so glad to see you. I was afraid something might have changed your mind. There was a boat went up the creek ahead of you, a white one. I just saw it going out of sight. Rodney, I wish you could see all the rain in your hair. It's like beads."

Through all that drizzle I had forgot to wear my hat. "Well," I said, "I'm glad to see you, too. The house looked so empty, I thought maybe you had gone. I am sorry I have got you so wet."

"I am sorry about all this rain," Brenda Sue said.

"It's all right," I said. "It's hardly your fault." Then I thought about what she had said about the rain in my hair, looking like beads, and it seemed to me that it must look pretty silly, so I ran my hand through it and rain scattered out from it and splashed on us both. "Rodney, the human sponge," I said.

"It was pretty," she said. "Honest. But now all you have done is mess it up. Come on to the house and you can comb it."

"I guess there is not much sense in our standing out here in this drizzle at that," I said, and then with both of us wet by this time, but with it not bothering us that I could tell, we walked on up to the house and went in. Then the screen door slammed shut behind us and the sound faded, and the next thing I knew I was standing in Brenda Sue's bedroom, because that's where the comb and the mirror were, standing bent over her little dressing table staring in the mirror at my own unexpected face, with, behind it, Brenda Sue's face, watching my eyes in the mirror while I watched hers, the light on the table shining up on our faces and making them look like we had both been caught somehow by surprise. And for a time I did the best I could, but with Brenda Sue right behind me, it was confusing, with our eyes looking at each other in the mirror like our own real eyes, but with our faces seeming somehow separate and with eyes of their own, seeing us looking at our-

selves, until finally I said, "Brenda Sue, do you have a feeling we are being watched?"

She laughed, and I watched her laughing in the mirror, laughing myself and seeing that, too, but noticing at the same time the way she lifted her head a little and the tip of her tongue showed when she laughed, back from her teeth, but showing, and the way little wrinkles formed at the corners of her mouth and how white her teeth looked and how red her lips. And then she stepped back from the mirror and her face was serious and pale and soft in the different light. "It's like we are being watched, at that," she said, "but there is no one here but us."

My hair was as combed as I was going to get it combed and I stood up straight and turned out the light below the mirror and turned to Brenda Sue. And what I thought was, And here we are in your bedroom, and we had better get out. But that was not what I said. I said her name.

The light in the room was the light of the rainy day coming in through the windows, and the quiet was the quiet of the rain. And for a time it was the same as it had been outside, except that the coolness of the rain was gone and the words we said had the sound of whispers, no matter how we said them, and the feeling of space around us was altogether different, as though there was hardly room for us to stand back now and then, even if we wanted to. But slowly it changed, as though the day got darker and the room got smaller, although this was just the way it seemed, while the change was real. Just standing there we slowly changed, as though we grew older and quicker and stronger and more certain, and without ever saying it, more single together in what was happening and what we felt, until the change was all that seemed to matter. But then I knew it could not go on just slowly changing forever, and I guess Brenda Sue knew it, too. "We had better go out on the porch," she said.

And knowing she was right, the sound of my voice surprised me. "No, not yet," I said.

Then the newness and difference slowed the change, and we

talked in whispers and admitted our surprise, and rested from it, side by side, even listening to the rain, and wondering when it had changed and we hadn't noticed. I told her how pretty I thought her dress was, and she mentioned again the sight of the rain in my hair. And I was glad I had said, "Not yet." "See?" I said. "There is nothing to be afraid of."

I believed it, and it seemed that Brenda Sue did, too. And then it was different again and the room got still except for the sound of the rain, and the change was more than it had been before and went on like the rain, like it had to go on, and could go on and on and on forever. And then Brenda Sue took my hand. "Rodney," she said, "we had better go out on the porch after all."

"It's all right," I said.

"But I'm scared," she said.

"What is there to be scared of?" I said.

She squeezed my hand tight. "I don't know," she said. "But I'm scared. I have never really liked a boy so much."

We had better go, I thought; we had better go, all right. "I have never liked a girl so much," I said. It was the truth, and it seemed right that I had said it, and everything seemed right again to me.

"Rodney," Brenda Sue said, "I can't help it, I'm scared. I have never been kissed lying down before."

"Honest," I said, "there is nothing to be scared of."

Then there was only the sound of the rain, just for one long minute, and then Brenda Sue pulled away. "Oh, Rodney, yes there is," she said.

And I felt the pounding of her heart and the pounding of my own, and I knew that she was right. And suddenly I knew that that was what it was, not the things people said, the trouble and worry and the awful things that can happen, not that to be scared of, but the pounding of our hearts, the bigness of that pounding, all the meanings of it, all unknown. And I finally had the sense to be afraid myself.

"You are right," I said.

We lay there awhile, listening to the rain, being quiet to-gether, and then we got up and went out onto the porch,

162

where we stood for a time looking down at the creek, watching the rain beat down into the water like it would never stop.

"When the rain lets up, I will leave," I said.

So we sat on the porch and talked and watched it rain, our voices going back and forth as steady as the rain itself, drumming on the roof above our heads. We talked about everything, mostly ourselves, but ourselves and everything else, as though the whole crazy world could someday be ours, even if not right now. And the rain kept pouring down, like a kind of company to us, as though we weren't altogether alone at that.

It wasn't a hard rain, but it was steady as the ticking of a clock, and finally, more and more, it was not so much a kind of company to us that I was waiting to have leave so that I could leave, too, as it was a reminder of time itself, time not stopping, time just drumming the minutes and hours away, while we sat and talked, as I stayed longer than I should have stayed, until both of us knew it, and until that was all we seemed to be talking about, that when the rain let up I would have to leave, if I was going to make it back to The Landing by noon the next day, the way I had promised.

But the rain didn't stop or even slacken. And I sat on the porch with Brenda Sue and talked, letting the rain be a kind of clock without hands for me, blurring time, but telling me that time was passing, even so, until finally the sound of the rain got to be too much, and I knew that I had to get up and go, rain or no rain.

Brenda Sue or no Brenda Sue.

I got up. "I have got to go," I said, "rain or no rain."

Brenda Sue got up and looked at me and then out at the rain and then back to me again. "If you have given Jack your word to be there," she said, "then I know you have to try. I'll go with you to the boat."

"You will get soaked," I said.

Brenda Sue only nodded, and then we stepped out into the rain and walked down the steps and down the long curving path to the pier, as though as far as we were concerned the sun was shining bright, as though the rain didn't matter at all. Then we were in under the little tin roof at the end of the pier and the sound of the rain was a different sound, like a kind of music almost, from the sound of the tin, I guess, and we stood and looked at each other not knowing how to say good-by or what else to say, either. Then we said good-by the same way we had said hello in the morning, both of us already wet this time when she reached and put her arms around my neck and I picked her up, and it was the same, the same surprise and wonder and almost disbelief, and the same wonderful happiness, the same realness, with even the same rain, and both of us wet. And when she stepped back from me all the serious, sad look that had been on her face was gone, and she was smiling as wonderful as I had ever seen her smile. And I knew what Brenda Sue must have known then, too, that we couldn't say good-by. Because what we were still saying and all we could say even now was hello.

So we didn't try. I untied the boat and got into it and looking up at her just before I picked up the oars and shoved off, all I said was, "Brenda Sue, I'm sorry if the rain and I have half ruined your dress; but I will never forget how pretty you look in it right now."

And I knew I never would.

I rowed off, watching the blue dress blur and fade out of sight in the rain. And when the last flash of Brenda Sue's waving hand was gone out of sight behind me, I turned and looked up ahead of me at the creek stretching out in the rain and then up at the sky overhead, and then I settled back and rowed.

16

I guess I had rowed along for a good half hour before I finally got the pictures of Brenda Sue to stop running through my head, the way a song will do sometimes, until as much as you might like it you are practically begging for it to quit. It just didn't make sense, rowing up a creek in the middle of the afternoon in a steady, miserable rain, soaked to the skin and with water running down from my hair into my eyes, half blinding me a good bit of the time, and all these pictures of Brenda Sue, smiling and laughing and serious and scared, changing all the time, but going on and on in my mind, clear as could be, and not making any more sense, considering the situation I was in, than if what I was doing was rowing along with a bunch of butterflies all flying around my head. But finally it eased off.

And instead of all those pictures of Brenda Sue, what slowly took their place in my mind was the single steady sight of the rain beating down into the water. That, and the thought of the creek, the whole long length of it, waiting for me up ahead. It did not add up to any sort of a pretty picture at all. The more I thought about it, the less and less pretty it seemed. If I still didn't know just where the Big Star turned into the Little Star, I knew, from experience, that between the two of them, they made up an awful lot of creek.

The last thing I had ever figured on was rowing up it in the rain. But that was what I was doing, and the longer I did it, the longer the creek came to seem to be in my memory. Without the rain, the distance alone wouldn't have bothered me too much, as the moon was better than a quarter-moon and was still rising early, and I could have rowed half the night by moonlight. But if the rain kept up until night came, then I didn't know if I could keep on rowing or not. Even without the moon, with just stars, I think I could have done it, because all I would really have to see would be the trees sticking up against the stars on both the banks. It might have slowed me, up where the creek got narrow, but I believe I could have done it. With the rain, however, and no moon or stars at all, I believed it would be slow going at best. Or impossible. But the only thing I could do was wait and see. And in the meantime, row. So I rowed. And the rain kept coming down like it never meant to stop. It was monotonous.

After about an hour and a half of it, it was worse than that; it was a pain. My shirt kept sticking to my back and my arms and rubbing my neck where I had got it sunburned a little, so finally I took it off, and would have taken off my pants, too, as they were nothing but a bother to me, weighing me down with water, but I did not feel like stopping to change into my bathing suit in the middle of the creek, and in the rain at that, like some kind of a nut. I figured I must have looked crazy enough as it was, just rowing along in the rain, although finally I got tired of the way the water kept running down into my eyes and I stopped rowing long enough to look around in under the tarp in the front of the boat and find my baseball cap and put it on. Which probably didn't do much to help make me look more normal, but it helped me to see anyhow. It's a bright red cap and sort of glows; but how I looked, to be honest, hardly mattered to me.

What mattered to me most of all was time. It looked like time alone—not the creek or the rain—was the thing most apt to run out on me. While everything else stayed the same. The rain made the same steady hushed sort of splashing sound in the creek, and the oarlocks kept making the same little off-key squalling sound, like a blue jay trying to sing, and soaked as I was, even the crease on my new grey, stay-pressed jeans stayed neatly creased, a strange sight to see. While all I did was row, and watch the east bank of Big Star Creek go inching past me in the rain, and now and then look up in the sky for a sign of light I never saw, seeing only the sky, dark and unchanged, and the rain slanting down from it in long quick streaks, like silver strings, dragging more rain down behind it. The only good thing about it was that it was cool, and I could row along at least feeling clean.

For the rest, what I felt was mostly foolish. I had stayed too long with Brenda Sue, and I had known it all along. But I had done it. And now, I knew, what I had to do was to row and keep on rowing, rain or no rain, night coming up or not, stars or no stars, moon or no moon. There was nothing else to do. The creek was long and The Landing was up at the end of it, and there was nothing going to get me there but my two long arms and my bent back and Mr. Haywood's boat. And without his cypress skiff, with nothing but a bunch of cans of food with half the labels soaked off, his newly painted white boat a good deal the worse for wear, and a number of holes poked in his tarp where we had fastened it to the oars for a tent—with all this, along with Jack's broken wrist, it seemed the least I could do was to try and get to The Landing on time. So that Mr. Haywood wouldn't have to just sit there and wait. For nothing. Just for me.

But even as I kept rowing along and the rain kept coming down and time moved along about as fast, it seemed, as the boat was moving slow, I could never quite get myself convinced that I was sorry about having stayed so long with Brenda Sue. I knew I should have been, but I wasn't, not even when I had finally become convinced that the darkness up in the sky and the spreading hazy light along the water was not just a sign of more and harder rain, but a sign of evening, of the light easing out of the day and of night and darkness on the way. I felt foolish and worse, knowing that there couldn't be any sensible way to row up a twisting creek at night in the rain, but knowing I would have to try it, even so. But I didn't feel sorry about the time I had spent at Byrd's landing. I couldn't believe it had been wasted.

And I was willing to waste the whole night if I had to, just trying to find my way on up the creek by instinct alone, if sight and all else failed, or by lantern light, if I could find some dry matches and get the lantern lit. But I knew I would never back down and start complaining to myself about the

167

time I had spent with Brenda Sue. Not even if I rowed all night in circles.

When you are watching the treetops against the sky, it can be surprising the way night can come and you still can see. At least you can see the treetops longer than you can see anything else. I found it out by watching. And slow as night comes, especially if you are watching for it, still, how fast it seems to come, too. Things just fade away, distant things first, like the sight of the creek up far ahead or back behind, then the details of things, so that the woods across the creek first blur and then look like a solid wall and then fade into the darkness of the creek, which has also gone dark, and all that is clear is the very tops of the trees, a kind of broken line running along against the sky, a little darker than the sky, and· nearer, although now and then you can lose it, and then you look around and it is dark everywhere, and it is night, and you have never really seen it happen. But it has happened.

Anyhow, when night finally came, it came slow enough to fool me, and yet fast enough to catch me surprised. I hadn't even lit my lantern. I had just kept rowing. And then it was dark, and the tops of the trees across the creek on the west bank seemed gone for good, and all I could see was the tops of the trees sticking up against the darkness of the sky close by, and I eased the boat in closer to the shore, wondering if this was as dark as the night was going to get or if I would lose the sight of these trees, too, and just end up lost, rowing along with nothing to go by at all except the feel of my oars dipping down in the water to prove I was still in the creek and going somewhere.

Then I noticed how the sounds can get loud on a creek at night, along with the less you can see. Right away, I started hearing sounds I hadn't noticed before, or the same old sounds I had been hearing started sounding more individual and clear. Even the sound of the rain coming down into the water. It seemed I could hear it all up and down the creek, splashing down with the soft easy sound of echoes, and then fading off to a sound almost like a whisper, so that I would strain my ears

168

to hear it from as far away as I could, as though just by listening I might be able to tell where the creek curved away, where it went to in the dark. And I heard the frogs and the other calling, singing sounds of things along the shore, and the noise they made rose up above the rain now and then and rang out across the air as clear as though the night was empty and still except for their singing. I could even hear things moving in the water, just the sound of something heavy, swirling the top of the water up ahead, or something making a kind of sucking sound, not a splash, not the clear slap of a fish that had jumped and slapped the water coming down, but the sound of something that had disappeared and had been big enough so that when it had sunk back down from the top of the creek it had sucked the water back down with it, loud enough to be heard. In fact, even with the rain, right after it was dark, I heard sounds from the creek that I had never heard before. It was alive with sounds. And if I couldn't see the different things that made the sounds, I knew they were there, all right. And listening, just rowing along and watching the tops of the trees and hearing the sounds that marked the shore, the frogs making all their different sounds along by the bank, and hearing the sounds out in the creek itself, the thought came to me that if I only knew how to do it, if I was only smart as an animal myself, by the sounds alone I might have been able to find my way up the creek without needing my eyes at all.

Then I ran the boat right into a bush. I had known I was close to the bank, but still, it startled me. It also knocked my cap off. How I did it I don't know, but I felt the bush bend back against my head and then spring loose, and I felt my cap fly off, and I guessed at which way it must have gone and reached out and down into the water and pulled my cap back out, without ever having seen it. I couldn't have been more surprised than if I had reached down and pulled out a fish, not seeing a thing. I sat there, hardly believing it, and then not knowing what else to do I wrung it out as best I could and put it back on my head.

It was funny how a little thing like that, losing my cap and then finding it again, could seem to give me a new kind of hope about the whole situation, as though things were not as much out of my control as they had almost come to seem to be. I still had my cap, anyhow; and I guess you might say that putting it back on and wearing it as wet as it was, silly as it might seem, somehow helped me to keep my head as well. I had drifted out from the bank, so I picked up the oars and started rowing easy, pulling more on the right oar than on the left, until I heard the boat go scratching along into the bushes on the bank again, only this time on purpose. Then I reached around in the dark until my hand caught ahold of a bunch of leaves and I felt around until I found the branch of the bush they were growing on, and I pulled the boat up close and held it there while I found the rope at the back of the boat and tied it fast, doing it more by feel than by sight. What I needed most of all was a light, and I did not want to be drifting around out in the creek while I crawled back in under the tarp and found the lantern and Jack's tackle box with the matches in it and got the lantern lit if I could.

I was surprised at how dry it was where I had stored the blankets up under the front seat, which was where the lantern was, too, and the tackle box when I finally found it. It took me a while, though, crawling around on my hands and knees, holding the tarp up with my back, pushing cans and stuff out of my way along the bottom of the boat until I got to the front of it. But I got the lantern lit with the first match I used.

The light of that lantern lighting things up all around me down under the tarp was like a kind of miracle, the way it changed things. I had never thought that a simple lantern light could look so bright. Then I crawled back out into the back of the boat and held the lantern up and looked around and saw the rain still coming down and the leaves of the bushes wet and shiny along the shore close by, and then I untied the boat and set the lantern down on the back seat and rowed out into the creek again and headed back up it.

Right away, from the minute the east bank was out of sight, which it was with the first good hard pull on the oars, I could see that my problem was far from solved. All that my nice

170

bright lantern did was to more or less blind me. It showed up the rain and a tiny circle of the creek around the boat, but that was all. Anywhere else that I tried to look, up into the sky or back toward the trees along the bank, or ahead of me or behind me, all I could see was a curtain of pitch-black night, as though all the lantern could do was light up a hole in the darkness, useless for showing me where I was, except to show me how deep and solid the rest of the darkness was around me.

Without the lantern, it hadn't really seemed that dark. Now and then I had been able to see the trees against the sky at least. Yet for a while I kept trying to row along as though the light was a help, and it did make the night seem friendlier somehow, if nothing else. But it wasn't long until I knew that, nice as the lantern light looked to me, it was making things worse than they had been before. I had to admit it. For all I knew, I might be rowing along straight for the west bank, or starting around in some stupid circle out in the middle of the creek. All I could actually see was the boat and some water. And what I needed to see was just about anything else.

I stopped rowing and let the boat drift while I looked at the lantern and then out at the darkness and tried to make up my mind what to do. I would lie if I said I wasn't disappointed and discouraged, both. When the light from the lantern had first flared up, all my confidence had seemed to rise up with it. I believed that the worst of my troubles were over. Now it looked as though I was right back where I had been before, except that now I had gotten used to the light, even if it didn't help. Yet for all the time I sat there thinking about it, I already knew that there was only one sensible thing for me to do, and finally I did it. I reached down and pressed the lever that lifts the lantern glass, and then I blew it out.

Then the dark was about as dark as I have ever known it to be. I could not see a thing. Not even my boat. All I could do was sit there blinking in the dark and wait to see if I was going to be able to see something again, anything again, or not. Then right off in front of the boat something swirled in the water so big and so close that it made the boat rock, and

171

for one long minute or two after that I not only sat there feeling blind and lost and helpless, but scared as well.

It was the sound of a bullfrog, back off behind me, that helped to get me using my brains again. I knew what a bullfrog was, and I knew he would not be swimming around in the middle of the creek calling out to some other bullfrog, but would be somewhere back along the shore. The sound had come from behind me, so one of the creek banks would have to be there. And from the distance of the sound, it would put me, I figured, about where I would have guessed I was; out in the middle of the creek.

So I eased the boat around and then the bullfrog sent his deep, low lonesome call straight out from the darkness ahead of me, and I rowed toward the sound as though it might have been a bell that had been rung, a signal just for me. And as I rowed I noticed that I could see the boat again, at least, and when I looked up it seemed that the rain had slackened and that the sky was not as absolutely dark as it had been before; so I turned and looked and clearer to my sight than they had been since the night had started, I saw the tops of the trees along the east bank, standing out against the sky.

There was no doubt about it; the rain was slacking off, and I could see again, better than I had been able to see before. I swung the front of the boat around and headed up the creek, seeing the treetops clear against the sky beside me, not as bright as with a moon or even as bright as it might have been with stars, but being something I could see and something to go by finally. Then far across the creek on the other side I saw a light up ahead, and then another, and I knew where I was. With all my trouble, I had reached the last long stretch of landings that according to Jack was as good a place as any to say that here the Big Star had finally become the Little Star Creek.

The lights sure looked good to me, and it was a lonely feeling to see them drop from my sight as I stayed near the east bank and watched the trees against the sky and curved around a bend and was on my way up the Little Star, with the lights of the landings and the Big Star left behind. The rain had gone down to little more than a drizzle again, and the sky seemed to grow even lighter as I rowed, making it easier and easier for me, and I wondered how, with no stars or moon, the sky could show a kind of light now, even so. And then I remembered that up above the rain clouds there was not only blackness and night but stars and a moon. It was almost as though I could see it in my mind, the low-hanging rain clouds, thinning out now, with high up above them the stars and moon shining down and lighting them up from above. And that is what I see, I thought, the light that gets through.

The way I went rowing on up the creek after that, more and more sure of myself and noticing the light getting brighter all the time and the rain almost stopped, it seemed to me that I had finally won out against time and the creek, or that I was on my way to winning. The line of treetops against the sky was as easy to follow as a line drawn on a map, and if sometimes I had gotten into a bend before I noticed it and had run into some bushes, it was easy enough to back off and look up ahead and get my bearings again. All I had to do was to stay fairly close to the east bank of the creek and follow wherever it led me.

And that was what I did and it worked fine. Until I rounded a bend and began to notice that something seemed wrong. The line of treetops I was following still looked right, but the sharpness of the curve I had followed, and kept following, seemed strange, as though I should have remembered it, but couldn't. So I kept my eyes on the treetops, but slowed down and kept rowing, until something really strange happened, and I stopped. I had noticed that the treetops I had been watching had stayed the same for quite a while, and they had never done a thing like that before. They were slow to change sometimes, but they changed. It was more or less the only sure way I could tell I was moving.

What was wrong was something I still didn't know, but I hadn't sat there for long without having figured out that I wasn't moving and hadn't been moving for quite some time. Then I reached in under the tarp and found the tackle box and got out the matches and crawled over the tarp to the front of the boat and leaned down and struck a match and looked down into mud. I stood there looking down at it until the match burned my fingers and went out. I had gone aground on a mud flat without even knowing it, just easing into it. And after that, I had been sitting there rowing away for nothing, going no place.

I crawled back over the tarp in the dark and sat down and looked up and waited for my eyes to get used to the darkness again, after the light of the match, and finally the line of trees came back into view, unchanged, each single treetop so familiar to me that I wondered why, with all the time I had spent looking at them, I had not bothered to do something bright about them, like give them names. I was disgusted with myself.

But I sat there until I had figured the whole thing out. I had followed the treetops along the east bank of the creek just the way I had planned, and I had followed them right on around and straight into Mud Turtle Creek and a good ways up it. I had known the creek was there, but I had forgot. And if it hadn't been for that mudbank that stopped me, I thought, I might still be following those treetops like an idiot. And then I finally thought, well, I am not lost, anyhow, just a long ways up the wrong creek and stuck in the mud.

Once I had figured it out, I could see there was no point in just sitting there feeling tired and stupid, and I stood up and shoved the boat free of the mud with an oar and turned it around and started back the way I had come. And somehow it didn't surprise me at all when the rain started coming down harder again and the light faded more and more in the sky. By that time, I think I expected it. I don't think it would have surprised me if it had started to thunder and lightning as well.

I had almost got dry, but soon I was soaked again. This time, the rain seemed colder, and more often than not as I rowed along I couldn't see a thing. I got so it hardly bothered me when I would go sliding into some bushes or bump up against a snag, although when I would back away from whatever it was I had run into, it was sometimes hard to remember which way the front of the boat had been pointing before. And when finally I must have gotten turned around and rowed the wrong way and ended up on either the same mud-bank again or another just like it, it hardly made me mad.

The creek had won out after all, and I knew it. And for a time I sat there feeling more or less like I wished it was all right for me to cry. But then I straightened up. Well, I thought, the mistakes were mine and here I am and there is no way to change it, certainly not by crying; anyhow, there has been enough lousy water in this night already. Then I looked around in the rain, not able to see a thing, and in my mind it seemed I could see the whole long creek stretched out somewhere behind me, the way I had first seen it and the way it was, and then the thought came to me: okay, so I have lost; but that long old creek has been there forever, while I am hardly sixteen damn years old.

So then I worked the boat loose from the mud again and got it turned around and rowed until I bumped into a tree sticking out from the bank, where I tied the boat for the rest of the night. Then I lit the lantern back under the tarp and put the oars in place and fixed up the tent the way Jack and I had fixed it before. I took off my wet pants and shoes and put them up on the fish well, and then I dried myself off with one blanket and wrapped up in a couple more, and blew out the light. Then I lay there listening to the rain. It sounded like it never meant to stop.

But I was just too tired to care.

17

It was enough to be dry and warm for a change and not to have to sit staring up into the dark and the rain looking for treetops that had disappeared from sight; I went to sleep quick. And I slept hard.

I guess that when I went to sleep I was more tired and discouraged than I would admit. The last thing I really remember was blowing out the light, as though I had blown out the last of my hope as well. All I could understand was that I was tied to a tree way up at the shallow end of Mud Turtle Creek, and that I should have been back on the Little Star, still rowing. There was nothing left for me to do but wait. And all I had really meant to do was to lie there listening to the rain and waiting for daylight; but I guess I just gave up.

Which was probably the smartest thing I had done in some time.

I don't know how long I slept, not more than a few hours, I imagine, but it sure made a change in the way I felt. I could tell it even before I was altogether awake again, waking up slow and easy and feeling the boat under me rocking a little and tugging at the rope that held it fast, slowly noticing that the rain had stopped and that everything was quiet, with just the boat moving slow and easy in the water, still holding me half asleep, even after I knew where I was. Then I opened my eyes and lay there awhile longer looking up at the tarp above my head, not really seeing it but just knowing it was there, close enough to touch, not being certain yet if it was daylight outside or still night, dark as it was in under the tarp, but not awake enough yet to care.

The first clear thought that came to me was that a heavy

tide must be running, pulling at the boat, and that that was what I felt, the tide moving past me. If it had been the wind, I would have heard it. But there was no sound at all. And then slowly my mind started working a little, although I was not really awake enough to call it thinking, but somehow I knew that if it was a good strong incoming tide that I felt, rocking the boat the way it was, then as nice as it was to just lie there half asleep, I had better wake up and get going. Because if I got back down to the Little Star soon enough, with a good strong tide behind me, I might make it yet to The Landing in time.

Yet it was hard to get all the way awake, even when it was clear to me that I ought to, that it was time; and I stayed where I was as long as I could, stretching and feeling my muscles slowly waking up, too, it seemed, like my body had been having a sleep of its own and no more wanted to get moving now than I did. But then the boat gave a tug at the end of its rope that I could not pretend I hadn't felt, and I gave up and rolled over and crawled to the fish well and threw back the flap of the tarp and looked out.

It was morning. And it was an incoming tide, all right, which had swung the back of the boat around facing east. So that what I saw was the sight of Mud Turtle Creek, stretching out long and straight in front of me and narrowing down in the distance, where it seemed to disappear right into a woods that was all that stood between me and a full and blinding sight of the rising sun. For a time I just kneeled there leaning on the seat and staring out at the creek and the woods and the rising sun as though my mind had gone blank, as though I hardly existed, as if I had lost track of myself altogether. It was as though the sight I saw was something I had never really seen before and was almost impossible to understand. I might as well have been crouched there staring out at a brand-new world. And then I realized I was hurting my knees and hardly breathing; and feeling almost foolish about it, I crawled on over the fish well and stepped out from under the tarp and stood up and looked around. And even then it took a while longer, just standing there and looking all around, to get the notion out of my head that either the world or myself, one of us, had more or less just been born.

I suppose all that it really amounted to was the fact that, having spent most of my life so far in cities rather than in woods, I had never actually seen a sunrise quite like this one before. That and the fact that having gone to sleep in a boat in the rain, tied to a tree along a creek where I was not supposed to be, with time running out on me and with the skiff I had lost still lost, I had honestly somehow not expected to wake up the next morning to anything great.

It was surprising, to say the least.

Yet I looked around and I had to admit that I had never felt greater in my life. And then I saw that I was lucky as well, because off back down the creek I could see the bend where Mud Turtle Creek joined with the Little Star. I had done better rowing back down the creek in the dark than I had known. I had almost made it all the way.

So I grabbed a can of tomatoes from the front of the boat and opened it and drank off the juice and threw the rest away, not wanting to waste time sitting there eating, and then I loosened the tarp and threw it up front and put the oars back in place and untied the boat and started rowing. Ten minutes later I was headed back up the Little Star and moving right along, rowing hard, with most of the creek still caught in the shadows of the morning, but plain enough to see, and the sun rising higher all the time.

It was the easiest rowing that I had come to yet, with no wind to hold me back and with the tide coming in strong behind me, low and rising, and judging from the high-water tide marks along the shore, having a good ways to rise before it was full and would turn and start back out. I was in luck, for a change. And I rowed along, hearing a fish jump now and then in the quiet or a bird singing off in the woods, and then everything would be quiet again except the sound of the water sliding past the boat and the sound the turning oarlocks made, sounding now like music in my ears.

By the time you could really say that the sun was up and it was day, I had reached and passed the clearing where Jack and

I had stopped at noon to eat, on our first day coming down the creek. And as late as we had left that morning and slowly as we had moved along, and had reached that clearing by noon, I was certain I could make it back up to The Landing with at least an hour to spare.

I rowed my way on up the long twisting part of the creek that went winding about through the cypress swamp as though it might as well have been the longest and straightest and quickest stretch I had come to, as far as the way I wouldn't let it slow me down. And then the rest of the way, past the place where I had lost the cypress skiff and then past the clearing with the PRIVATE, KEEP OUT sign, and then finally past the island, more and more I let myself slow down, as the need for speed was finally gone. And it was well before noon, with the day not even good and hot yet, when I rowed up easy to The Landing and made the boat fast.

For a time I sat there resting in the boat and looking around at the empty clearing, and then I started unloading. I stacked everything out in the open, about where Jack and I had stacked it to start with, the morning we left. It made a good-sized pile, but although I did the best I could with it, it all looked a good bit the worse for wear, especially the sight of all those cans with their labels soaked off. Then I spread out the tarp to dry in the sun and took a couple of blankets back to some shade at the edge of the clearing and stretched out on them, ignoring the mosquitoes, and went to sleep.

I sure was tired. But I had made it.

I never even heard the truck drive up. What woke me up was the sound of Jack's laughing. I had gone to sleep flat on my back with my cap pulled down over my face, and I pushed the cap back and looked up and there was Jack, looking down at me and laughing, and when he saw my face he started laughing even harder. I noticed his wrist was in a cast. "See," I said, "I told you it was broken. I didn't find the skiff." I had no idea what he was laughing about to start with, but when I said this, he slapped himself on the leg with his good hand and started laughing all over again, and then Ellen was standing there beside him, just smiling at first, and looking kind of curious and worried, and I smiled back and said "Hello," and Ellen started laughing, too. Then I slowly stood up, stiff from sleeping on the ground, and Mr. and Mrs. Haywood came up and stood there looking at me, Mr. Haywood just staring for a time and then slowly shaking his head from side to side, as though he did not quite believe what he saw.

"You poor boy, you," Mrs. Haywood said.

I could not have been more surprised than to hear her say that. "Except for not finding the skiff," I said, "I feel fine. I have just been resting from the trip." Then I looked down at myself, wondering if there was something wrong in the way I looked, and I saw that I was not too clean and was barefoot and without a shirt, and that some of the red color in my cap had run down in the rain and had left some red marks still showing down across my chest and stomach, as well as more or less changing the color of my jeans from grey to a kind of dirty red. When Jack saw me looking at myself he started in laughing again, and when I looked up Mr. Haywood was laughing, too, in that quiet way he has. "I guess I must look a little funny at that," I said. "I got caught in some rain coming up the creek last night." Then I looked around smiling to see if that was what everyone was laughing about, and this time even Mrs. Haywood had to laugh.

"I have heard of it raining cats and dogs," Jack said, "but never blood."

"It was this crazy cap of mine," I said, and I took it off, and for just a second everyone was quiet, and then Jack let out a laugh so loud it made me jump, with Ellen making a wild kind of squeal at the same time and then turning away and grabbing Mrs. Haywood and hanging on to her still squealing and laughing and acting like she couldn't catch her breath, while Jack started jumping around the clearing, slapping himself and laughing as though it was about to choke him, until he turned and saw me looking at him, and then he lay down on the ground and laughed. Even Mr. Haywood turned away from me, laughing, when I looked at him. In fact Mrs. Haywood was the only one who still seemed able to stand there and look me in the eyes. "Mrs. Haywood," I said, "I get the impression that I am somehow responsible for the fact that most of your family seems to be having fits right now."

"Rodney," she said, "I'm sorry, but I wish you could see your face." And then Ellen got control of herself and let go of her mother and grabbed me instead and still laughing dragged me with her over to the pickup and stood beside me while I stood there and got a good look at myself in the rear-view mirror on the side of the truck.

No wonder they are laughing, I thought. I guess the most startling thing of all was my hair. It was supposed to be blond, but it was as solid a blazing red as if it had been dipped in paint, while my face looked as though it had been used to mop up whatever red paint that had been spilled. Only my nose had escaped. It looked as white and unnatural sticking there in the middle of my face as the painted nose of a clown. Then I looked away and they were all standing around watching me. "Well," I said, "I went away a boy, but as you all can see, I have come back a clown." Then Mr. and Mrs. Haywood stood there smiling and shaking their heads at me and Jack and Ellen stood back and did the same, almost as though I was as much to be wondered at as laughed at. "Watch," I said, "and I will do a funny thing." And then I walked past them all and walked down to the pier and out to the end of it and off it and into the creek. I could hear Jack laughing again before I hit the water.

One thing about Jack, it sure is easy to make him laugh. I got as cleaned up as I could by swimming around in the creek, but all the way back to The Hill, all Jack would have to do was to look at me from the other side of the back of the pickup and start in laughing again. For some reason, it didn't bother me at all. Just out of stubbornness, I was still wearing my red cap. Ellen rode in the back with us, and for a while she tried asking me about the things I had done after Jack had been brought home from the Byrds', but I was too tired to give her much in the way of answers, and I guess she could tell this, but every now and then I would see her looking at me, as though she was still wondering about it all.

The first thing I did back at The Hill, after helping unload the pickup, was to take a hot bath. And the next thing I did, tired as I was, was to write a letter to Brenda Sue. Which I had promised I would do. It wasn't much of a letter, I guess, but she had wanted a picture of me so I sent that, too. The first picture of myself that I had ever sent to anyone. I hoped that the letter would explain it.

Dear Brenda Sue, I wrote. Well, I have made it back okay, none the worse for wear, and like I said I would do I am writing so that you will know that I made it back in time to make connections with the Haywoods as planned. I certainly enjoyed meeting you. It was a pleasure to meet your parents, too. They were certainly nice to Jack and me. As you can see, I am rotten at writing letters, but you mentioned a picture of me, which you will find enclosed. It's the only one I have. I am the one in the middle holding the basketball, and never mind about those other four. Ha! Ha! I am not as skinny now as when that picture was taken. I am tired from the trip, so this letter will be short the way a stupid letter ought to be, but all that I am leaving for you to read between the lines is something I hope you will understand. I will say one thing, however, and that is about the name your mother calls you, Babe Honey. What I want to say about it is only that your mother is sure good at names! All your names. Brenda Sue Babe Honey, I mean. I guess it is none of my business, but I could not think of better names for you if I tried. And that is all I will try and say in this letter, except to say that I am not joking when I end this letter the way I end it now. I mean it.

Then I wrote, Love, and signed my name, Rodney Gerald Blankhard. I got a stamp from my uncle and waited for the mailman and gave him the letter, and then I went in and stretched out on the bed and slept until supper. Once, Jack came over and came pounding up on the porch and stood there saying my name a few times, but I was too tired to talk, and he finally went away.

At supper, I ate like a horse, and then I went back to bed again. I could not have stayed awake if I tried. Aunt Vera made Jack let me sleep the next morning, and even with the heat on that back porch, I slept until noon. On The Hill, a thing like this is news, and when I got up and started moving around, everyone sort of treated me like I was just getting over some kind of a sickness. Even Jack kept asking me how I felt. I felt fine. I had never felt better in my life.

And I guess I got everyone convinced of that, because that night I sat on the Haywoods' porch, with my uncle and Aunt Vera there, too, having come over to thank Mr. Haywood for bringing me back from The Landing and to see about paying for his lost skiff, and Jack and I told them about our trip together down the creek, and then they all stayed, my uncle and aunt and all the Haywoods, while I told them about my part of it alone. All that seemed right. I don't think I have ever talked so long at one time in my life. I was surprised at the details I remembered and at the way it all came back to me. I would have thought it was something I could hardly ever tell to anyone, that it would be impossible to remember or to explain, yet once I got started I could hardly stop. And they all laughed some now and then, but the nicest thing about it was that they listened like they cared. Like it was interesting even. And then I came to the end, and it was quiet, and I felt embarrassed at having talked so long. Then Mr. Haywood stood up and said, "Rodney, I will not have your uncle pay one penny for that old lost skiff of mine. You did a fine job of looking, and that is all that matters. And maybe someday you will find it yet."

Then it was quiet again and my uncle stood up. "I will not insist," he said. And that was all he said, for once, and then he and Aunt Vera left and Mr. and Mrs. Haywood went back inside the house, and soon Jack got up and went in, leaving just Ellen and me.

"Well," I said, "I guess I am probably keeping you up, so I had better go."

"No," Ellen said. "I waited on purpose. There are still a few things you haven't said. I can tell."

"About the creek?" I said.

"About Brenda Sue Byrd," Ellen said. And then she laughed. "And I don't expect they will be said now, either. Rodney, you may have fooled the others, but you haven't fooled me. Tell me—" and she laughed again, the old teasing sort of laugh I knew so well, only now I wondered if all along it wasn't a laugh that had always been meant for us both, and not just for me—"are we still good friends?"

I thought about it and I knew she was teasing me, all right, but I finally thought of the right answer, one she might even think was smart, coming from me. "Like we are brothers," I said.

And then, feeling that that might have sounded smarter than I meant it, I reached out in the dark and found her hand and squeezed it and she squeezed mine back and I knew it was all right. Then we sat there and laughed. And soon after that we said good night and I went home.

What I did for the next few days was to finally teach Jack how to work my Star Roamer set. I would never have thought that I would actually lose my interest in it, but I did. I would tune in Radio Free Cuba and they would be just as mad at the U.S.A. as they had been the last time I listened to them, but I could not convince myself that what I was listening to was the inside facts or even the most important things about Cuba. And it was the same with most other countries. I just stopped believing that I was really listening to the world. Except maybe for shrimp-boat captains. Listening to them, I could still get hooked. But to Jack, once he learned how to work the set, it was a whole new world at his finger tips. He would sit there, half tuned in on England, just sweating with excitement. He even tried talking like an Englishman. It was awful, but at least it was different.

It was Wednesday when the letter came from Brenda Sue. It was longer than I would have expected. What she wrote was this:

Dear Rodney, Thank you for the letter and the picture. You do not look skinny. You look nice. I am sorry about the other four boys. I have enclosed a picture, too. The house in back is

184

our house, and the little dog is dead. Or lost, but I think dead, because I know he would have come back to me if he could have. His name was Scamp and I loved him. I guess you should not say you love an animal, but I did. Anyhow, the picture is not of Scamp, but of me. It was taken some time ago, too, like yours, and I have grown since. The dress is that same old blue one, though. I have never met a boy like you before and your letter was not a stupid letter at all and I hope you will come back. I am sorry it rained like it did after you left. I am not sorry that it rained though. You will have to read between my lines, too, as I am probably the worst letter writer in the world. But I will write back if you do. Your letter was the nicest letter I have ever got. I wish I could tell you how nice it was. I hope I will hear from you soon. In the meantime, I will keep my eye out for that skiff you lost. It is bound to be around here somewhere. I will sign the same as you. And I mean it, too.

It was signed, Love, and then her name, just Brenda Sue.

I spent the rest of the afternoon after Brenda Sue's letter came trying to answer it. I could never seem to say just what it was I meant to say. But I tried. Jack, jumping around behind me at the Star Roamer set, trying hard for China, didn't make it any easier.

As far as I am concerned, and as that set is concerned, Jack can have it.

Even as far as the whole world is concerned; for all I care, Jack can have that, too.

Who needs the whole world?